THE
LOST SCROLL
OF THE
PHYSICIAN

Secrets of the Sands

The Lost Scroll of the Physician

SECRETS OF THE SANDS

THE
LOST SCROLL
OF THE
PHYSICIAN

ALISHA SEVIGNY

TORONTO

Publisher and acquiring editor: Scott Fraser | Editor: Jess Shulman
Cover designer: Laura Boyle
Cover illustration: Queenie Chan
Printer: Webcom, a division of Marquis Book Printing Inc.

Library and Archives Canada Cataloguing in Publication

Title: The lost scroll of the physician / Alisha Sevigny.
Names: Sevigny, Alisha, author.
Description: Series statement: Secrets of the sands ; 1
Identifiers: Canadiana (print) 20190117079 | Canadiana (ebook) 20190117087 | ISBN
    9781459744295 (softcover) | ISBN 9781459744301 (PDF) | ISBN 9781459744318 (EPUB)
Classification: LCC PS8637.E897 L67 2020 | DDC jC813/.6—dc23

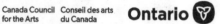

We acknowledge the support of the Canada Council for the Arts and the Ontario Arts Council for our publishing program. We also acknowledge the financial support of the Government of Ontario, through the Ontario Book Publishing Tax Credit and Ontario Creates, and the Government of Canada.

VISIT US AT

 dundurn.com | @dundurnpress |  dundurnpress | dundurnpress

Dundurn
3 Church Street, Suite 500
Toronto, Ontario, Canada
M5E 1M2

Ancient Egypt:
The Second Intermediate Period ...

1

THE COBRA HISSES IN STRIKE POSITION, forked
tongue flickering, hood flared wide. Its icy, flat
stare remains unbroken except for the vertical
blink of its eyes. My fingers move up and down the
long wooden reed, covering some holes and releasing
others, as the notes float up and up. Gaze locked with
mine, the snake slowly undulates from side to side and
my body relaxes a fraction as our spirits entwine. A
crowd has formed.

This is what I want.

Vendors walk toward the spectacle, attention
drawn. People point and laugh, momentarily distracted from the oppressive heat of midday as they
move in closer for the show. My eyes don't leave the
snake's, but I know Ky is weaving through the carts,
lifting a plum here, palming a fig there, taking whatever is most easily on offer. Hopefully he'll find some
bread, maybe some nuts and fruits, though there hasn't

been much variety of late. My ears strain for shouts, an exclamation of "thief!" over a rumbling stomach, but the crowd is as mesmerized as the serpent.

Snake charming is not common knowledge here. My father taught me the art, just as he taught me to read and write, also not so common — especially for a girl. But he believed that learning and knowledge bestow power on their possessor. Unfortunately, all his knowledge and power were not enough to keep him and my mother from being killed.

Pain blooms raw and fresh, as if the cobra has struck my heart. Has it only been one moon since they were stolen from us?

Focus.

I need to focus or the snake's *Ka* will break with mine. Then I will not be so safe. Though safety is mostly an illusion, I think.

Higher and higher, the snake rises in the air, out of the basket woven with grasses picked from the banks of the Nile by my own hands. Ky's and mine. His are much faster. I pray to Amun they are fast now and try not to think what will happen if they are not. A fruit vendor, bald and fat, clothes stained with the juices of his wares, thrusts a finger in my direction and jeers.

"The snake is drugged. See how slow it moves."

I do not stop playing to tell him the snake is moving slow because it is entranced. Also, the heat of this day would make any creature sluggish. My heckler himself is sweating, a hairy, meaty arm coming across his dripping brow. Others begin to murmur, debating the state of the cobra's consciousness, attention wavering.

This is dangerous.

I move the reed in dizzying circles, notes coming faster. The snake follows the instrument, not taking its eyes from the wand, regarding it as a predator. It does not matter what tune I play, as the reptile can sense the sounds but not the individual notes. Those are for the audience, and so I try to make them as pleasing as possible. Unlike the fat man, I do not want my clothes splattered with rotten fruit.

There is a noise at the back of the crowd. My body tenses. A dog barks, then barks again. Time slows as the fat man turns, upper body twisting as he cranes neck over shoulder, double chin coming last, pointing in the direction of the commotion.

Please don't let it be Ky, please don't let it be Ky.

But Amun must be sleeping because there is my brother, scrawny arm held tight in the grip of an angry woman, dark hair frizzing around her shoulders like pregnant storm clouds. She is yelling and my brother's face is pinched and scared.

My foot shoots out, kicking the basket over. Screams erupt from the crowd as Apep goes slithering off in search of cooler and calmer surroundings. The flash of regret at the hours of now-wasted training is quickly replaced by an intense fear that my brother could possibly lose the arm the woman is clutching.

Or worse.

Running through the panicked crowd, Ky and the screeching woman disappear in the churning masses. Frantic, I whirl in all directions, desperately trying to catch a glimpse of the pair.

A dog barks again and I look in its direction, eyes landing on the fat man.

"Don't let him go!" he shouts, enraged. Following his gaze, I see the woman with my brother.

"If you were not so lazy and distracted, thieves could not steal so easily!" she yells back. I realize she is my heckler's wife. He thunders toward them, one hand on the large knife at his side, sun glinting off the deadly blade. For a fat man he is quick as a crocodile, with a grin twice as evil. I dart under arms and around unwashed bodies, coughing on dust kicked up by sweaty feet.

"Sesha," Ky cries, catching sight of me.

"Release him," I say. The woman sneers at me in perfect imitation of her husband, who is only seconds from reaching us.

"I don't think so." Her lips twist in a cruel smile as her nails dig deeper into Ky's arm, making him cry out. "He is going to pay for what he took."

"He has nothing." I pray she will not lift his tunic where the cloth sack is tied around his skinny waist. The fat man is almost upon us, knife gripped low. My mind races for a way out and comes up with nothing. I cannot leave Ky.

Then the dog is there, growling deep in its throat. It stares menacingly at the woman.

She takes a step back, unsure, pulling Ky with her. "Call off your dog."

"He is not mine to call."

"Liar."

And then the man is also there, lunging for me. I go boneless like Apep, and slip through his hands. He lets out a roar, rotten breath enveloping me as he fumbles for the knife. Reaching my brother, I grab his arm and pull with all my strength in the opposite direction. The man is on his knees, scrambling for his knife in the dirt. Tugging harder, I yell again at the woman to let go. She will not. She is too strong.

The dog lunges forward, jumping up on her front, teeth snapping. She screams, hands coming up to protect her face, releasing Ky so suddenly that I stumble backward and we fall hard to the ground. But only for a second.

Jumping to his feet, Ky extends a crescent-marked arm to help me up. We race through the market, dodging around stalls and people too preoccupied with their own lives and the possibility of a snake underfoot to pay much attention.

I hear both the man and the woman shout behind us, but we are lightning, darting into shadows that even the sun's rays cannot dispel. When at last we are sure of our safety, we stop, hands on knees, breath coming fast and hard, tracks of sweat running down our dusty faces. It is several minutes before we speak.

"I'm sorry, Sesha," Ky says, distress in his dark brown eyes. "My hunger made me careless."

"Do not apologize for being hungry, little brother." I ruffle his brown hair, curly like our father's was. He brightens.

"Look." Untying the cloth satchel at his waist, he lets the tattered sack fall to the ground. Out rolls a fig, some grapes, a few berries, and one overripe plum, conjuring with it the smell of the man's decaying teeth. My stomach turns.

"Well done." I gesture to the food. "Eat. I am not hungry."

"Are you sure?" Picking up the fig, he has it in his mouth before I can nod. He needs it more than I. Noting the dark circles under his eyes and the pallor of his face under skin coloured by the sun, I gesture to him to sit as we lean back against a pitted wall behind one of the temples.

"Apep?" he says between ravenous bites, juice dribbling down his chin.

"Gone," I say, and he lowers his eyes. "Back to the riverbank where she'll be much happier."

"But … all the time we spent with her …" There's a slight tremor in his voice.

"I can find another snake." I pat his back and smile to let him know I'm not upset. "Another brother may not prove to be so easy."

He holds out some bruised grapes. "Have some, Sesha, they are delicious."

I oblige, knowing he will not relent until I eat something. We finish the food together, leaving only the mushy plum, which Ky pockets. A rustling sound to our left has us on our feet, heads swivelling in its direction. The dog from the market trots around the corner and we relax, slumping back against the wall. It walks up to Ky and licks his face, making him giggle. It nudges me next with a wet nose and I scratch its pointy ears. There's a chunk missing from the left one, an old injury leaving the skin soft and smooth.

"Do you know this dog?" I ask, curious as to where it came from.

"He saved us," my brother says, laying his head on the lean torso. "He is ours now."

"Just what we need." I sigh. "Another mouth to feed." The dog barks and a hind leg comes up to scratch vigorously behind his torn ear. "And fleas."

2

"**D**O YOU THINK PHARAOH knows we're alive?" Ky asks for the dozenth time, leaning back against crumbling sunbaked brick, tossing the plum high up in the air then catching it, over and over again.

"I imagine he might have come to that conclusion," I say, adding a few twigs to our small fire, "seeing as how our bodies were never found."

We have made our way back to our nightly refuge: an abandoned storage hut, thatched roof half fallen in, three decrepit walls. We face the missing fourth, which — while breezy — allows for a wondrous view of the palace rising up in the night. It feels like a life ago that we were once free to roam its halls. I was a different person then.

"And you really think he ordered Father to be killed?" His voice catches, tripping over far too much anguish for a boy his age. He misses the plum and it falls to the earth with a *splat*. The dog looks up.

"I'm not sure," I say, permanently filled with despair at the thought of my father's friend being capable of such betrayal. But how else to explain what I saw that night? Guards fleeing from the house, right after the blaze broke out. Guards bearing the pharaoh's personal crest. Shuddering, I shake my head to rid myself of the awful memories. "It may have been just a terrible coincidence."

Yet something whispers in my ear that it was not. Still. I have no evidence, no proof, and even if I did, what can I do? All I can do is keep my brother safe and out of Pharaoh's vast reach, on the chance that he did have something to do with that night's events. Not an easy task.

"Why would anyone want Father dead? He helped so many people." Ky pets the dog, who has wandered over to sniff at the flattened plum. He has taken to calling him Anubis. I'm not sure if the jackal-headed god will be honoured or offended by his mangy namesake.

"I've been trying to figure that out myself," I admit. "There is just one thing that stands out in the months leading up to the fire. That big project he was working on."

"The scroll?" Anubis, seeming to dislike overripe plums as much as I do, leaves the fruit and lies down. He rolls over, offering his belly for Ky to scratch.

"Yes." Our father, consumed with the transcription of a very important document, would not go into detail of its contents, only that it would have great implications for Egypt, and the rest of the world. All those late nights at the temple and the secrecy surrounding the papyrus have stirred up my suspicions, like desert winds to the sand.

More and more I am coming to think that his and Mother's deaths were not an accident. Her sweet voice and translucent honey eyes come to me now, as water fills my matching amber ones. I blink it back as the dog gets up and trots over to me, his own moist eyes, one brown one blue, examining mine. His expression is so human that I wonder if there is not a bit of the god in him.

The growing desire to find out exactly what happened to my parents swells now, bursting over the banks of my heart and flooding my body like the great river after the rains. I vow to Ra to discover the truth. This last moon I have been focused only on surviving and caring for Ky, while grieving Father and Mother. But I will find out. For their sakes and for mine.

Anubis cocks his head and blinks, as if to approve my decision, then goes to lie beside my yawning brother, who, exhausted by the day's events, curls into a ball on the sand, just as Ra's golden vessel finishes its journey across the sky. Removing the cloth wrapped around my shoulders, I lean over, covering Ky with it. And for his sake, most of all. For though I do not know much about the papyrus my father was working on, I do know it has the power to save my brother's life.

A noise has me starting awake, bolting to an upright position. My heart beats fast, shooting energy through my body. Anubis is also awake, alert and standing, looking into the night as though expecting something or someone. Ky has come uncovered and is shivering. Pulling the cloth up over his small shoulders, I sit back, no longer tired. Anubis comes to sit beside me, perched on his haunches, still vigilant. Scratching behind his ear and staring into dying coals, I recall Father, a few moons before the fire, talking excitedly to Mother about the scroll. From my bed, I remember pulling down the blanket, sleepily eavesdropping.

"Incredible discovery … the Great Imhotep … only surviving copy … save our Ky …" I see him clearly in the night, both then and now. Back to me, hands animated, he picks up my mother and spins her, his kiss making her giggle like a young girl. The fire crackles and her laugh floats away on the wind.

I need to find out more about the papyrus. If it is as important as Father deemed, it could be a clue to what happened to my parents. And if he felt it could help Ky, then all the more reason, for every day my brother grows more ill. Looking at him, face gaunt in the shadows, I am struck by a fist of guilt. Am I doing the right thing keeping us hidden from the pharaoh?

We could be in the palace right now, warm, bellies full. Ky would be playing with his friend Tutan, one of the young princes. I could resume my studies. But if Father was keeping the scroll quiet, then there must have been a reason. Perhaps there was someone he did not trust at court or at temple? Anubis stiffens, cocks his head, and whines.

"Peace, Anubis. Dinner was hours ago and it is only the discontentment of an empty belly that has me thinking such thoughts." But the dog bristles again and I feel the hairs on the back of my neck lift in response. This past month has taught me to trust my instincts. I look around, wincing at how exposed the fire makes us. But I'd wanted Ky to be warm. Never mind that, now. We need to get out of here.

"Ky, wake up." I shake my brother gently. "We have to go." He murmurs and turns over and I shake his shoulders more vigorously. "Ky, wake up, we need to leave this —"

"And what is it we have here?" A harsh voice, jarring in the night, has me leaping to my feet and Anubis growling. Ky is awake, rubbing bleary eyes that blink at the three figures now blocking our view of the palace, closing in on us.

The guards step closer. "We heard there were thieves in the market today, causing a disturbance," the biggest one says, voice rough and full of malice. "Seems like someone's been upsettin' the vendors these past weeks. Takin' things that don't belong to 'em."

"What in Amun's name are you talking about?" I say in my boldest tone, glaring at the three soldiers. "My brother and I have done nothing wrong."

The big one, who seems to be their leader, spots the spoiled plum and picks it up off the ground. "Now, why don't I believe you?" Anubis barks and he rounds on the dog. "And look at this. There was mention of a dog. A dog they described as lookin' a lot like this one."

"Who are 'they'?" I challenge, backing up to stand in front of Ky, now fully awake and wide-eyed with fear.

"That would be us," says a nasty voice from the shadows. A familiar meaty arm reaches out to grab Ky, pulling him into the dim light of the dying coals. The triumphant vendor towers over my brother and me. His frizzy-haired wife stands behind him, eyeing Anubis warily. "This is the boy. He and his filthy brother stole from us." I don't bother to correct them.

"And your only proof is a plum?" I borrow my manner from Princess Merat, daughter of the Great Royal Wife and the haughtiest of Pharaoh's offspring. The giant guard raises an eyebrow over a crooked nose that's been broken more than once. He looks familiar.

"And the dog." The woman steps forward, eyes spewing venom. "It attacked me. The mongrel must be killed at once."

"No," shouts Ky, making a move for Anubis. The vendor throws him to the ground.

"You have no evidence to support your claim," I appeal to the crooked-nosed guard, who seems to be listening at least, desperation replacing some of my haughtiness. "It is our word against theirs."

The guard steps forward, eyes narrowed. "That's some fancy talk for a flea," he says, spear coming up to poke at my rags. I force myself not to flinch, holding his gaze. "Exactly who are you, Flea?"

Remaining silent, I sidestep his spear and hurry over to assist Ky, who is slowly getting to his feet. He is pale and trembling.

The vendor steps toward us, emitting malevolence along with his foul breath. "Let's throw them and their dog in the Nile and be done with the thieving demons."

I look around. We are trapped. There is no hope for it. Taking a deep breath, I commend our souls to Ra and peel back the layers of grit that have settled on me these past few weeks.

"I am Sesha, Daughter to Ay, Great Physician and Chief Scribe." Whirling, I stare at the broken-nosed guard, injecting as much force as possible into my tone, fully invoking the proud princess. "And I demand to see the pharaoh."

3

"**S**ESHA, WHAT ARE YOU DOING?" Ky whispers.

"I don't know," I whisper back. What have I done?

"This is outrageous!" the vendor's wife snaps. "She is obviously lying."

Crooked Nose circles me, examining my features more closely. I know he will see tawny eyes peering out from a dirty face, tangled brown hair that, when washed, glints with gold, or so my mother was fond of telling me. A straight nose, proud like my father's. I stick it high in the air now, to show my disdain at his examination. This comes easier than expected. Merat really does have quite the range of expressions.

"I am not lying. I'm sure the pharaoh has been looking for us." I gesture to my brother and myself. "He will be most angry if we are not brought before him." I do not know if this is true, but it's the only thing I can think of to buy some time, and hopefully avoid landing at the bottom of the Nile with one of these crumbling bricks tied to our feet. Regardless of whether Pharaoh had something to do with my parents' death, I'll take possible treachery over certain drowning.

Crooked Nose spits and turns to the other guards. "We better take them in." They look unsure but are too well trained to argue.

The vendor and his wife are not. "We need to make an example of these vermin," the vendor demands. In the dark it is all too easy to imagine the purple-red stains on his clothes as blood. "Or they will multiply like locusts, a plague on the marketplace."

"That is not going to happen today," Crooked Nose barks at the vendor, then fixes me with a gimlet eye. "Though if she is lying, you can have her, her brother, and the dog for wasting my time."

I swallow. That does not sound like an idle threat.

The palace rises up before us, opulent and enormous, a shining white beacon of light. Despite my misgivings, a feeling of coming home spreads through my body. Ky and I grew up here; running through Father's chambers, playing with the pharaoh's many children. Perhaps I am wrong and he had nothing to do with Father's death. Perhaps it was completely unrelated to the papyrus. Perhaps it was a tragic accident. We draw nearer to the palace, Ky practically vibrating beside me, Anubis on his right.

"Do you think Tutan will remember me?" he whispers, relieved to be on our way to warmth, food, and people who were once friends.

"We have only been gone one moon" — I smile down at him — "Not only will he remember you, he will be praising Amun for returning you safely to him." Ky is beloved by everyone at court, but especially by young Prince Tutan, Merat's brother and current heir to the throne. My brother radiates a sweetness that makes all who meet him want to protect him on sight. I glance over my shoulder.

Present company excluded.

The guards walk behind us, spears at their sides, not drawn, so not a particularly hostile escort. This has my spirits lifting. The vendor and his wife had continued to argue with the guards, but after a few threatening jabs with a spear, slunk away into the shadows, disappearing with the first light of morning, robbed of their vengeance.

For now.

"This way," Crooked Nose commands, leading us into the high-ceilinged hallway, limestone painted lavishly with gold sparkles in the sun's rays. Upon entering the main hall, an aching weariness spreads through my bones, and not only because of the interrupted night's rest. After a month of surviving moment to moment, worrying about our next meal, potential snake bites, my parents' death and my brother's worsening condition, my body is finally saying "enough." I stumble, almost collapsing onto the granite floor with exhaustion. It is in this unfortunate position that Pharaoh strides into the room, his people behind him. Though he is not tall, he is broad and emanates a powerful pull that draws one in. His dark eyes are kohl-lined; right now they show concern.

"Sesha, gods be praised, is that really you and Ky?" I attempt to stand, Ky helping me up, and we bow before him.

"Yes, My King," I say, voice hoarse.

"I cannot believe it" — he blinks — "nor can I recognize you under that tangled mop and those layers of filth. You must be cleaned up at once. But first some food. I can count your bones, those that are visible beneath the dirt." He claps and Wujat, Grand Vizier and former High Priest, steps forward. Where Pharaoh is thick and barrel-chested, Wujat is whip thin and tall, but emits no less strength than the man whose kingdom he helps run. He was also my father's friend, and would often seek his council. It is a balm on my spirit to see him.

"Sesha, Ky." His voice is warm. "I am so glad we have found you. Tell me, children, why did you not come to the palace straight away?"

Ky looks at me, one hand on Anubis, who has been permitted to enter with us.

"We were … confused, Oh Holy Wujat," I say. It is truth enough. "We did not want to be a burden on you, My Lieges."

"Nonsense," Wujat says and Pharaoh nods. "Your father was a great man and served the kingdom well. How could you think yourselves a burden?"

"Sorrow can make one behave in odd ways." Queen Anatmoset, Great Royal Wife, steps forward in her golden headdress, as beautiful as always. "The poor children were probably frightened half to death. To lose their parents in such a tragic manner." She shakes her head, raven hair swinging along with the jewels dripping from her person as we bow before her. "I am so very sorry for you both," she says, her thickly lined black eyes taking in our disheveled states.

"Thank you, my lady," I murmur. Though nothing but kind, Queen Anat, as she is called, has always intimidated me. Descended from a long line of kings, it is said she often advises her husband and Wujat on state matters. Pharaoh inherited the throne when he married her.

She gestures for two of her servants to attend us. "See that they are fed and washed," she commands. Ky slips his hand into mine, which does not go unnoticed. "I will have the new physician attend to you both, as well."

I flinch. So Father has been replaced. I suppose it was inevitable. Members of the large royal family need someone to care for their health. "Thank you, my lady." The attendants lead us away from the great hall and I exhale, unaware I've been holding my breath.

"That wasn't so bad," Ky whispers as we walk down the grand corridor.

"No," I whisper back, careful to not let the attendants hear. "Yet I still cannot shake the feeling that we've just walked into a nest of vipers."

Ky squeezes my hand as we head for the physician's chambers at the end of the palace. "Lucky for us, you're a snake charmer."

4

I AM STRUCK BY THE FAMILIAR smells the instant I enter the physician's chamber. For the second time in mere hours, moisture assaults my eyes, which I close, letting the scents of my father and his work wash over me.

"Everything is exactly the same," I say, looking around. Anubis sniffs at some bowls in the corner. Ky lets go of my hand and walks over to the counter, picking up the pestle from the mortar Father used to grind up herbs and medicines.

"It would be silly to change things when they work so well where they are," a voice says. Ky fumbles the instrument but manages to catch it before it crashes to the floor, hastily returning the utensil to its place on the shelf. "I am Ahmes. You must be Ky," the man says, then turns to me. "And Sesha. I am glad to hear you are both alive and well."

"Thank you." I bow, inspecting my father's replacement. He is tall, head and body shaved, as is the custom. His brown eyes are warm and they look out at us with concern. He is much younger than I expected.

"And who is this?" He looks at the dog.

"Anubis," Ky says.

"Ah," he nods. "There is food being brought for you. Would you like to wash first or later?"

"Now, please," I say, eager to remove the grimy film of sand that's covered every inch of my body for the past month.

"Very well. And you, Master Ky?"

Ky's stomach grumbles loudly. "Food, please." Anubis barks his agreement.

Ahmes smiles. "Of course. Sesha, you know the way to the baths, I presume?"

"Yes."

"We will wait here for you." He gestures to the large table at the other end of the room. A serving woman walks in carrying a tray laden with food and drink. The delicious aromas make my mouth water and I almost change my mind about bathing first. She passes me, placing the tray on the table, and I see her nose wrinkle, nearly imperceptibly, except a month on the streets has sharpened my powers of observation.

Never mind. Bath first.

Emerging from the pools feeling better than I have in a very long time, I dry myself with the cloth provided.

"Sesha." It is Merat, the princess whose manner I evoked when dealing with the guards. "Welcome home." She places a clean robe on a chair beside the pool.

"Thank you, Princess." I bow, aware of the generosity of the pharaoh in letting me use the family baths and the honour of Merat bringing me the robe herself, without her usual condescending expression.

"I am sorry about your parents." Her words are sincere. "Your father was a good man. I will never forget how he saved Tutan." The young prince once suffered a severe reaction to a scorpion bite and Father saved his life.

"He loved Prince Tutan like another son," I say, tightening the cloth around my body, self-conscious of my now clean — but presumably still bedraggled — appearance. Her eyes flicker over my hair.

"I will send Nebet to you," she says. Nebet, personal dresser and attendant to the elder princesses, is a sorcerer with her combs and kohl pots.

"Thank you, Princess," I say again and she nods, leaving the baths as regally as she came in.

Has a month on the streets addled my senses? Maybe my original assumption about wandering into a vipers' nest is wrong. So far everyone has been nothing but kind. Perhaps they truly do feel sorry for us. I sigh, putting on the clean linens Merat brought.

I need to find the scroll. Not only did Father believe it could help Ky, it might also contain information that could either condemn or clear the royal family. At the very least it will spare me the pains in my neck from constantly having to look over my shoulder.

Ky belches loudly as I walk into the physician's chambers, better prepared for the onslaught of emotion that comes with entering my father's former domain. He is alone, except for Anubis.

"Where is Ahmes?" I glance around for the physician.

"He was called to attend one of Tutan's sisters. She has The Fever."

"Which one?" I ask.

"Little Tabira."

Poor thing. The Fever is especially ruthless on children. It can come and go without warning, alternating between burning up and bone-racking chills. "May Amun be with her," I say and my brother nods solemnly. It occurs to me that Ahmes's departure has provided an opportunity.

"Ky," I urge. "Help me search for the scroll."

"What? Now?" He glances around the room.

"Yes. Perhaps Father hid it in here." Walking around, I look on shelves, peering under counters, in drawers.

Ky gets up and explores the room, looking with me. Father also taught him to read and write and though he is only ten, he can decipher most texts with ease. "Do you know what it looks like?"

"Like a scroll?" Stopping in front of a desk, I stare down at a surface overflowing with papers. Picking one up, I scan the document. "A Treatment for The Malady of Fever," I say aloud.

"You can read."

I jump. Ahmes stands in the doorway. I wonder how long he's been there.

"Yes," I stammer, cheeks growing warm. I hope he attributes it to the baths. "My father taught me."

He studies me. "Is there any particular reason why you're riffling through my things?"

"Don't you mean our father's things?" The sharp words escape before I can stop them. Lowering my gaze, I bite my lip.

"They are mine now, Sesha" — his voice is gentle — "but if there's something you'd like to remember him by …" Relief floods my body. He thinks I'm looking for sentimental trinkets. This could work in my favour.

"Actually," I begin, doing my best to keep my tone casual, "there is one papyrus I'd like to have. Maybe you know of it? My father was working on it before he died." Hazarding a glance, I see an unsettled look cross his features.

Too much.

He is familiar with the document. Cursing the loss of my angle, I press onward. "It is something I was helping him transcribe. It would mean so much to have it back."

If Ahmes did not shave off his eyebrows, one would rise now. "Are you referring to the Great Imhotep's treatise on surgical traumas?"

"Yes." I hold my breath. That must be it.

"The document is gone," he says, abrupt.

"Gone?" Ky echoes.

"Yes," he says, voice terse. "No one's seen it since your father died. It's assumed it perished in the fire …" *Along with your parents* hangs in the air.

No. That cannot be. Father did not keep his documents at home.

"What about the temple?" I suggest.

Ahmes closes the door to the chambers and walks over to me. "What about the temple?"

"That is where he did most of his work. That and here." I gesture. "But the temple is more peaceful. It is where he preferred to carry out his academic pursuits."

Ahmes pauses, then, "I believe the temple has been thoroughly searched."

It sounds like I am not the only one looking for the papyrus. I wonder again at its importance. "Who searched the temple?"

"I did," Wujat says from behind.

5

I WHIRL AROUND. The pharaoh's Grand Vizier examines me thoroughly, making me wish for something slightly more substantial than the linen robe I'm wearing. He must have come in through the back entrance.

"Not personally, of course." He waves a hand. "I had several of my men go through the temple from bottom to top."

I am sure the priests loved that. Obtuse guards pilfering through hundreds of holy documents and generally wreaking havoc. Wujat should know better, having held the office of Most High Priest before his duties as Grand Vizier had him delegating it to another, namely my father.

"And they knew what they were looking for?" I say cautiously, a plan forming in my mind. Ten ankhs to one his men can't read.

"They came back with several documents, yes. But none was the correct one. Your father was waiting until he'd finished the transcription before revealing it and presenting it as a gift to the pharaoh. The papyrus is reportedly attributed to the Great Imhotep, and is the only known copy." Wujat starts pacing. "Ay believed it contains knowledge that has been lost to us, increasing its already inestimable worth."

"How did it remain hidden so long?" I can't help but ask. But I know how vast and complex the catacombs are under the temple, where things can and do stay hidden for hundreds of centuries.

Wujat does not answer. "The priest who originally discovered the document was not convinced of its authenticity. He showed the scroll to your father one night and Ay thought otherwise. He persuaded the priest to let him study and transcribe it. The manuscript is over fifteen hundred years old and in desperate need of preservation."

"And what of the other priest? He does not know its location?"

Wujat hesitates. "Brother Qar has since … departed for the afterlife. Most unfortunate."

Or convenient, depending on who is asking. Either way, this means there are no remaining witnesses to the scroll. Not that Wujat knows that …

"Does Your Holiness think it may help if you had someone who knows exactly what the scroll looks like?" I venture, mind racing. "I worked closely with my father and accompanied him to the temple many times."

That in itself is true.

"Are you saying you would know the document we speak of upon sight?" Wujat stops pacing and turns to face me, crossing his long arms.

"Yes." That part is not. "If you would allow me, I could go to the temple and resume my studies where Father left off. I could talk to the other scribes and be your eyes and ears. I can find the scroll, I swear it."

Wujat says nothing, bringing his hands behind his back in a formal stance. "I will speak of this to Pharaoh," he says, after what feels like eternity.

If Pharaoh does indeed have anything to do with the fire, I am not so sure how well this will work in my favour.

"Does Your Grace think this is necessary?" I say, a month in the sands having increased my daring, as well as my apparent capacity for intrigue. "After all, you said yourself, Pharaoh is most fond of surprises. What if you were to return the scroll to him after he thought it lost forever? I'm sure he would be most generous with his appreciation."

Wujat thinks for a moment. "That is an interesting thought."

Ahmes clears his throat. The physician is standing beside my brother and Anubis, the trio quietly observing our back and forth. "And what of Ky?" he asks. "Will he join Sesha at the temple?"

Ky looks depressed at the thought and I hide a smile. He does not love his studies as much as I do, finding them boring and tedious.

"If it pleases the pharaoh, I'm sure Ky is most anxious to resume his friendship with Tutan. Perhaps he can help tutor the young prince?" I say.

Ky brightens and Ahmes also smiles. "I could also use someone around here to assist me in a few matters. Would you be interested, Ky?" I shoot him a meaningful look, which he does not miss. I can search the temple and Ky can be the eyes and ears here in the palace.

"Thank you for the honour, Ahmes." Ky bows.

The door swings open. "Ky!" yells a familiar voice.

"Tutan!" The two friends race toward each other, embracing like long-lost brothers.

Tutan pulls back, face looking like he's just smelled something very bad. Which he has. "You smell like a rotting donkey's corpse in the heat of the midday sun."

Ky grins. "Sorry, Tutu. I have not had the opportunity to bathe in such fine perfumes as yourself, this past moon."

"You have certainly been bathing in something," Wujat murmurs, waving his hand in front of his face.

"Come, friend, let us get you clean." Tutan gestures with the practised imperiousness of one who is destined to be king.

Ky looks to us and Wujat nods his dismissal. "Come, Anubis," he says to the dog, who obliges, following him out the door.

"Where did you find this ugly beast?" I hear Tutan ask as they depart. Ky murmurs something in response, voice echoing down the hallway.

Wujat turns to me. "Sesha, I have decided to bring the matter of your … studies before Pharaoh." I gulp. So much for surprises. "Eat now, and join us in the great chamber when you are finished. We will be waiting."

"Yes, my lord."

Wujat nods at Ahmes and leaves us.

"Thank you for offering to take Ky under your care," I say to him, going to sit at the table where Ky ate. The delicious smells wafting under my nostrils have my mouth watering and I tear into the bread, suddenly ravenous.

"It is not purely unselfish. I do need help around here." He pauses and I sense there is something else he wants to say. Trying not to inhale the bread in one swallow, I wait. "Your father was my teacher. He was a brilliant man and I respected him very much. I would like to do what I can for his children."

The bread forms into a hard lump in my throat and it is all I can do to try to choke it down. Ahmes must sense my emotions because he turns, busying himself with cleaning his instruments. "Your brother has a condition, yes? An excess of fluid inside his skull?"

The cup pauses at my lips. "How do you know this?"

"Your father spoke of it to me."

"Why?" I am as blunt as the tool he is storing in its casing.

"He wanted my opinion on whether he could be cured."

"And?" My food is forgotten.

Ahmes remains silent. Then, turns to me. "I don't know." Now I am silent. "That document which you seek," he says, "it is of my opinion that it holds Ky's best chance."

A thought occurs to me. "Ahmes, will you do the surgery?" He looks surprised at my question. "If we find the scroll, can you save Ky?"

"It will be extremely dangerous," he says.

"You said you respected my father and that he was a brilliant man. You agree with his theory that the scroll could somehow aid in the operation." At least I hope that's what he believed. "I know he would do it himself if not for his …" I gesture, unable still to say the word. Once uttered, it will become irreversible. "You also said you wanted to do what you could for his children. You can do this." I hold his gaze, voice impassioned.

Ahmes sighs. "You should assist Pharaoh with his speech-making, Sesha."

"Does this mean you will help us?"

"Very well." He nods. "As long as you are aware of the risks."

"Thank you," I breathe. "You are a good man, Ahmes."

"And you are much too thin. Finish your dinner," he says, with a pointed look at my plate. "You will need physical as well as mental strength if you are to be attending school. The hours are long and some of your fellow scribes may not be so pleased to have a girl studying alongside them. Nor some of your teachers, for that matter."

"Will they hate me?" I ask, all at once uncertain. I had completed most of my training at home with Father. And when I did attend temple, he was always with me.

"Let us hope they will judge you justly, based on your own merits," Ahmes says.

"By who else's merits would they judge me?" I say, puzzled. "Father's?"

Ahmes looks directly into my eyes. "How much do you know of your father's life at temple before he came to work for the pharaoh as his Chief Physician?"

I shift under his piercing stare. "I know he was brilliant, as you said. That he was a great teacher and doctor, as well as head scribe for a time before he was called to care for the royal family." Father had implemented several changes at the school, reforming many of the temple's teachings in regards to medicine. While much emphasis had always been placed on proper spells and incantations for healing, the discovery of the scroll had further inspired him to equally value rational observations and scientific principles. After my father used information contained in the papyrus to cure Pharaoh's top military general of a severe injury, one which the gods could not help, Pharaoh had also been motivated to embrace these changes and brought him into the palace as Royal Physician.

"Your father was much favoured by the king," Ahmes walks to the door. "There will always be men who are jealous when the stars illuminating their paths shine not as bright."

The idea that Father was not beloved by all does not fit with my image of him. Then again, there is the small matter of his death. I suppose he could not have been popular with every soul.

Before I can ask Ahmes to explain further, he takes his leave. "You will have at least one friendly face at the temple," he says. "I teach there once a week. And make no mistake, my expectations for you are high."

"That is if Wujat can convince Pharaoh to let me attend in the first place," I say, just as a servant walks up to the doorway.

Bowing before Ahmes, he looks directly at me. "Pharaoh requests that you join him in the main chambers."

I get to my feet. It appears I am about to find out either way.

6

WE WALK DOWN THE gleaming hallways and I am thankful for our echoing footsteps, which cover the thudding of my heart. I must convince the pharaoh it is in his interests for me to join the other scribes at temple. There I will be free to search for the scroll. I am more certain than ever that the document is my best chance for saving Ky and finding out what happened to my parents. Thoughts swirl around my head and before long we stand before the entrance to the grand hall. I catch a reflection of my snarled strands in the polished marble and sigh, the breath sparking a smouldering ember of vanity a month of rough living has not entirely snuffed out.

Just then, Merat exits from a doorway and glides toward us, a servant scurrying behind her.

"Sesha, there you are" — she nods — "I have summoned Nebet to attend to you."

"But she is wanted before the pharaoh, Princess," the servant escorting me says. I look to Merat.

"I will occupy my father for a few moments. Go," she commands and turns to enter the grand hall, my thwarted escort following meekly behind. One does not argue with a princess.

I follow Nebet over to a nook in the corridor. There is a window and light streams in, illuminating the wizened woman's face. She sighs and shakes her head, walking around me, muttering to herself.

"Where have you been sleeping, child, with the beasts?" She sniffs me, as if searching for further proof. Taking a small bag off her shoulder, she digs out various lotions and potions, setting them on the sill. Reaching in further, she pulls out a wooden comb sporting a myriad of vicious teeth. Pouring scented oil from one of the bottles into her hands, she rubs them together, coating my tresses with the pleasant-smelling fragrance of almonds. Tears fill my eyes. My mother loved rubbing almond and safflower oils into our skin, and would massage both Ky and me with them when we were younger, to ease us into sleep.

"Why are you crying, child? I have seen worse." Nebet picks up the comb and stands back, calculating her plan of attack.

"I miss my mother." I'm not sure whether it is her maternal ministrations or the fact that someone is caring for me in some small way that leaves me feeling vulnerable, blurting out my heart's sorrow to an almost-stranger.

She clucks her tongue again, matter-of-fact. "Our mothers never leave us. The love she bore you has suffused itself into every pore of your body since the day you were born. Feel it in your bones and blood and remember her often. Now." She comes at me with the comb. "Brace yourself."

Blinking back fresh tears, these ones from Nebet's yanks and tugs, I pinch my cheeks and straighten my robes.

"That is as good as we are going to get in such a short time." Grabbing my hands, she inspects the torn fingernails and calloused palms. "Come see me later and I will finish what I started. For now, you are presentable enough."

She gestures to my escort who has remained waiting outside the grand hall and he nods, opening the large door before me. Taking a deep breath, I follow him into the room. We go unnoticed by the pharaoh; he is deep in counsel with Wujat. Merat is talking to Queen Anat. Other familiar faces dot the room. Men and women of the court and servants mill about, attending to the needs of the Sun God's representative on earth and his family. People are eating and drinking while royal musicians play their instruments, providing a backdrop to the overall hum of the room.

Merat catches my eye and gives a small nod; my confidence is bolstered by her unexpected, but welcome, support.

"Sesha!" Queen Anat exclaims. "That is much better; you look almost human again. You were quite feral earlier, my dear." Luminous stones hang from her headdress, her hair and makeup exquisite. As Great Royal Wife she must appear beautiful and immaculate at all times, even on just an average day at court.

"Thank you, My Queen." I bow low. She claps, and another servant appears with a tray. Even though I just ate, my mouth waters at the aromas wafting from the extravagant dishes set before her.

"Sesha." Pharaoh's voice booms, startling me out of my drooling stupor. "Wujat has informed me that you wish to attend temple, to study with the other scribes."

"Yes, My King." I swallow. "My father was training me to become a doctor, like him. I have spent most of my thirteen years learning the medical arts."

"Is that so?" Pharaoh asks, surprised. "I find it most curious that a lady such as yourself would be interested in such a gruesome occupation. Wouldn't you rather be one of the singers at temple with the rest of the young girls? Or a handmaiden to one of the princesses?"

I hesitate, not sure how receptive Pharaoh is to the idea of a woman doing a job reserved primarily for men. While not unheard of, it is not so common for females to become doctors.

"I have a talent for healing, Your Highness," I finally say. "At least that is what my parents used to tell me." Though I know it in my heart to be true. There are many times I would aid Father with his patients and in their diagnosis and treatments. I also attended births with him as midwife. It seemed to put the women at ease. Countless times my small hands were able to manipulate areas that Father's were not during the precarious nature of childbirth, where the unexpected could, and often did, happen. Looking at the royals, I summon my most winning smile, inwardly praising Nebet and her pots and combs. "Besides, my liege, I fear the gods would be most appalled at my singing voice."

Wujat chortles and Queen Anat raises a thick charcoal brow. "Come now, Husband," she chides, lifting her goblet in a sweeping gesture. "What of the great physician Peseshet? She was much respected, overseeing an entire body of female doctors. They advanced much in the way of birthing and children." She takes a drink of her wine, the servant instantly at her side to refill her glass, which she permits.

"Of course, you are right, my goddess." Pharaoh's voice is soothing. "I did not mean to suggest Sesha is incapable because she is a girl. Only that she might enjoy more … lighthearted pursuits."

"Nothing would make me happier than continuing my studies, if it pleases Your Highness," I say, as firmly as I dare. Along with finding the scroll. I contemplate how to broach the subject, but thankfully Wujat comes to my aid.

"Sesha mentions she is familiar with the document her father was working on before his … accident." The Grand Vizier turns his body, speaking so only Pharaoh and Queen Anat can hear, but I, too, am able to make out his words. "It would be helpful to have a pair of eyes and ears in the temple for the express purpose of seeking it out. I have no reason to believe any of the other scribes are actively keeping it hidden, but one does have to wonder at its stubborn refusal to be found."

"You will know what to look for, Sesha?" Pharaoh asks, finally taking his eyes off his stunning queen.

"Yes, My King." I do not mention that I have never seen the document up close.

"That is good." His tone is serious. "It is of utmost importance that the scroll be found immediately."

"But why?" I blurt out before I can stop myself, then lower my eyes. "Forgive my impertinence."

"It is all right, Sesha, I have several daughters" — Pharaoh's tone is dry — "and more than a few wives. Though none as fine as the Great Royal One, of course." He nods at Queen Anat, who graciously inclines her head to him to acknowledge his compliment.

"Wujat mentioned it may have been written by the Great Imhotep?" I say, tentative.

"Yes. A document of not only untold historical importance, but with immeasurable practical value, as well."

"The scroll we seek is reputed to be a most comprehensive manual of military surgery," Wujat says, steepling his fingers. "We have reason to believe it documents a variety of injuries received in combat. Fractures, wounds, dislocations; it could be of incredible value to the upcoming campaign."

"Campaign?" The hum of the room seems to quiet; the music lessens and time slows as the pharaoh looks from Queen Anat, to Wujat, to me.

As if making up his mind about something, he clears his throat and lowers his voice. "The scroll is our best chance of mitigating the ill effects any battles might have on our people. Sources tell us there is an invasion coming, Sesha. We may be going to war."

7

WAR.

I shiver. Thebes holds an uneasy truce with the Hyksos at Avaris. The foreign rulers had taken over the north delta and flourished there these past years. Some, like my father, see the benefit in trading with them and learning new skills and technologies. Yet there are many Egyptians who feel that they should be eradicated from our lands. The simmering tension has always been there, just waiting to bubble over like a pot left too long on the fire. Perhaps that time is now upon us.

"Your skills will be much needed, as well," Pharaoh continues. "Especially if you are anything like your father."

"I have heard from the women she has great talent as a midwife," Queen Anat says. She waves her goblet at the musicians and they pick up tempo, the hum restoring to the room.

"It is decided, then." Pharaoh stands, as do the the others. "Sesha will attend temple with the other scribes and continue her training." Lowering his voice, he looks at me. "She will also be our agent in seeking out the missing scroll. Can you do that for us, my child?"

"I would be honoured, my lord." Relief at accomplishing the first part of my task whisks the dread of imagined battles from my body, though it is laced with uncertainty about my new status as, essentially, a spy for the pharaoh. However, I am now one step closer to saving Ky and discovering the truth behind my parents' "accident," as Wujat calls it.

"Good. I pray to the gods you do not fail us," Pharaoh says. The hint of *or else* hangs between us and I gulp down some much-needed air, having neglected to breathe these past few minutes.

Bowing low, I retreat from the trio, feeling like I've been dismissed.

Merat appears by my side, leading me out of the main room. "You will live in the handmaidens' quarters. They are by no means luxurious, but they're clean and quite comfortable."

A month of shivering in the cool desert air has me thinking the handmaidens' quarters sound entirely blissful.

"I would also like you to teach me to read," she adds.

I look at her. "Your Highness does not know how?"

She shrugs. "I had no desire. My destiny is to be a good match for my father to marry off. But since the passing of my sister Nefertiri, I am thinking I would like to have other options."

I remember Nefertiri, the eldest of Pharaoh's daughters. She died in childbirth, as so many women do, the babe shortly after. At best, there is a fifty-fifty chance of survival, though Father and I tried our hardest to increase those odds. Despite labour being a miraculous experience, it can also be a devastating one. I myself have no wish to get married, although I am of age. Marriage leads to babes and based on what I've seen, those may very well lead to death.

"Sesha!" Ky shouts, racing up to me in the high-ceilinged hall, voice echoing, Tutan and a sopping Anubis at his heels. "We were giving Anubis a bath, but Mau came in and he jumped out and chased him all over the palace." The boys are breathless with laughter, colour high in their cheeks. Anubis barks joyfully, shaking himself off.

"Who is Mau?" I ask, thinking of some poor servant being terrorized by the four-legged fiend, in addition to the two-legged ones.

"One of my pets," Tutan says, looking around. "He's around here somewhere."

"Where is your tutor?" Merat chides. "Letting you two roam free through the halls? What of your lessons today?"

"Ky helped me finish my work," Tutan says. "Besides, he and Anubis very much needed a bath."

I look over at Ky. With his dark hair plastered to

his head, his condition is slightly more noticeable. Despite this, he looks better than he has in weeks. He notices my examination and self-consciously pulls his fresh robes tighter around his body. "I am fine, Sesha," he says. The colour in his cheeks confirms his words and I nod.

"Good news, Ky. I will be attending temple to continue my studies." Despite the circumstances, I cannot keep the grin from my face.

"Gods be praised, my sister." Ky throws his arms around me. "Now you can leave me alone and let me play in peace." He turns to Tutan, rolling his eyes. "Even when we were begging on the streets she would have me write out scripts in the sand, so as not to forget them."

I'm about to retort when a wriggling feeling under my robe has me hopping around in circles, frantically patting at something crawling in the cloth. A small green lizard falls to the floor and scurries off for safety. Anubis lets out another joyous bark.

"There he is!" Tutan exclaims to Ky. "Mau must have fallen onto Sesha when you hugged her." He chases after the lizard, who has disappeared through the same doorway Merat came out of earlier, followed by Ky and Anubis. The dog looks back at me apologetically before bounding off. There is a high-pitched scream followed by more excited shouts and barking.

Merat looks at me, still patting myself wildly to make sure there are no other creatures making themselves at home on my person, her lips twitching. "Brothers can be most vexing, don't you think?"

"Quite," I manage, adjusting my robes into as dignified a fashion as possible, and we walk down the halls of the place that is to be my home. For now.

The handmaidens' quarters are beyond opulent compared to where Ky and I have been squatting this past moon. Unmarried women from the Royal Harem come here to serve Pharaoh's immediate family. The large, airy room is currently empty, as everyone is about their tasks for the day. Fatigue pours over me like water from a jug, and I struggle to stay on my feet as Merat shows me to the woven mat that is to be mine. It is all I can do to keep from flopping on it. Her words buzz in and around my ears like a pesky mosquito. "… start lessons … soon … Sesha?"

"Yes, Your Highness?" My bleary eyes tear themselves away from the bed.

She gives an acknowledging smile and I am struck by how much like her mother she looks. Queen Anat had four children. Nefertiri, who died at seventeen, fifteen-year-old Merat, five-year-old Tabira, and nine-year-old Tutan, destined to be pharaoh one day. "Rest now, Sesha. Your glazed expression reminds me of my brother when he is being lectured by his tutor."

"Thank you." I bow and she turns to leave.

"We will commence my training soon."

"As you wish, Princess." Nodding, she leaves. Collapsing onto the mat is like sinking into the plush feathers of a thousand ibises. Before my eyes even close, I feel myself descend into oblivion.

Waking, I blink, momentarily disoriented. Used to hovering on the periphery of sleep, I find it remarkable what a warm bed and the absence of worry about the safekeeping of one's body can do for the quality of one's rest.

It is night and I am not alone in my quarters. A few girls titter off to the side of the room and I wipe at the drool on my cheek self-consciously, patting down my hair.

"Greetings." I nod at the curious faces, some familiar, most not. I used to have a few friends at the palace, but it all seems so long ago now. Mostly it was Father and me, learning, studying, working together. Up until the last few months before his death, we'd been inseparable, unless his duties at temple and the palace demanded otherwise.

"So the gods have returned you from the dead, Sesha." A tall girl steps forward. I try to remember her name; it starts with a *K*?

"Yes … Kewat." The name comes to me and I smile. But it is not returned.

"I wonder what you have done to find such favour with them as to survive this past moon?" she says, raising a brow. "Or with Pharaoh and his family, for that matter."

I'm unsure if I should apologize for being alive or what I have done to earn her resentment. She makes my appearance in the quarters and at the palace seem a personal affront. The other girls form a small cluster behind her. One steps forward. She is small, like a bird, with light brown eyes.

"Sesha's father was much loved and respected by Pharaoh," she says, voice high and breathy. "It is only natural he wants to care for his children."

Or is it just a convenient way to keep a close eye on them? Regardless, I am grateful to my defender. She, too, looks familiar. Her words disperse the group and she flits toward me as the others go about their duties, some leaving to wash, others murmuring to each other as they adjust their beds to their liking.

"Peace to you, Sesha." She bows. "Do you remember me?" Her voice is gentle, curious.

"Bebi?" I say, the name appearing on my tongue.

"Yes," she chirps, hands coming together. "You and your father saved my mother when she was in childbed with my sister."

I remember her more fully now, fluttering anxiously around the room during her mother's labour. "The baby was turned." It had been a difficult birth.

"But you and your father brought her safely into this world, without much loss of Mother's lifeblood."

"The gods guided our hands." I smile at her. This one is returned. "Why would you think I would not recall you?"

"It is said that the shock of your parents' passing caused you and your brother to forget who you were." She cocks her head at me. "Why else would you wait so long to return to the palace?"

Why else indeed? My smile freezes in place. *Be careful, Sesha.*

8

"SO THAT IS WHAT people are saying?" I address her comment about the shock of my parents' death addling our minds, keeping my tone light. I am not sure whether to be offended at the suggestion I'd lost my wits, if only temporarily. However, I suppose it *is* better than the alternative reason: that I suspect someone at the palace may be capable of murder. And though Bebi seems kind, let that nugget get out and I will be sleeping somewhere a lot less comfortable than the handmaidens' quarters. "I should have known it would take mere hours for some story to circulate."

"Is it true?" Bebi asks, curious.

"My parents' death was … very traumatic," I say. It is not a lie. "I do not even know where they are buried." I hope that they made it to the afterlife. Their bodies were probably not in much shape for the trip. Tears fill my eyes and Bebi gives me a sympathetic pat on the back.

"I do not mean to upset you, Sesha. We will speak no more of this." She sits on the mat beside mine. "I sleep here. So if you need someone to tell your dreams to in the morning, I am here."

I offer her a watery smile and a "thank you," refraining from adding that she would likely not want to hear them.

I turn over to face the pale moon shining in through the small high window. My hours of sleep have left me restless and famished again. I also feel the ingrained urge to check on Ky. He has rarely left my sight this past month and his absence is like the severing of a limb. Shivering, I think of the vengeful vendor and his wife clutching Ky's arm. We had been lucky. If it weren't for Anubis … As if summoned by my thoughts, the click of toenails on the floor announces his approach.

"Hello, friend," I whisper to the dog as he trots toward me, tongue lolling. "Can you take me to Ky?" No doubt he is sleeping safely with Tutan, somewhere within the harem of women and children. But the need to see him resting soundly for myself has me getting out of bed and following the dog, tiptoeing past somnolent handmaidens, out into the cool hallway. Torches flicker in the darkness, lighting our way. Though I mostly know where we are going, I am grateful for the company.

Deep voices float toward me and I duck behind a statue of one of Queen Anat's ancestors, heart thudding. Wandering the palace late at night unaccompanied is something mainly concubines do and I have no wish to be mistaken for one. Anubis slinks back into the shadows beside me.

"And you are sure this is a sound idea?" Pharaoh's usual commanding tone is uncharacteristically dubious. Footsteps echo down the hallway as they draw closer to our hiding spot.

"She may know something," Wujat answers as they pass by. Shrinking back against the wall, I try to make myself smaller than a speck of sand. "It is imperative we find the scroll and we are running out of time. Even now there are reports of enemies at our borders, and even in our midst. A battle is imminent, Your Highness. We need to be prepared."

"The Hyksos are a warrior people," Pharaoh says. "We will need to proceed with caution. Perhaps there are ways they can be placated while we continue our search."

Wujat makes a noncommittal noise in his throat. "We need to show our strength. Egypt has languished too long under these barbarian invaders."

"The priests will not like Ay's daughter poking around their quarters," Pharaoh says. "I have heard talk of much friction between him and the others …"

I swallow, my constricting throat the only muscle moving in my entire body.

"Leave that to me," Wujat says, murmuring something else that I do not quite catch. Pharaoh gives a low chuckle and I strain my ears harder to hear.

"… And how are the food supplies?" Pharaoh inquires.

"Dwindling." Wujat's tone is frank. "The last harvest was poor, and the one before it barely mediocre. We have enough for the next few months but let us pray the gods see fit to bless us this season. One more bad harvest will be cause for serious concern."

So that explains the recent lack of variety in the marketplace. Though, based on my last few hours here it is clear that the palace has yet to feel the pinch. And who or what did Father have friction with? The priests?

"The people must not know," Pharaoh says. "I do not want to give them reason to worry; my guards say there is already some unrest in the village. I have my hands full with these pesky Hyksos as it is …" The voices fade as the two men disappear around a corner.

Exhaling, I emerge from my hiding place, Anubis with me, our shadows dancing along the walls. I consider the overheard conversation as we continue noiselessly down the corridor. My thoughts spinning, Anubis and I turn several more corners until at last we reach the large chamber that houses the younger royal children and those who care for them.

Poking my head in, I see bodies curled on every surface. Lesser wives wrapped around their babies, toddlers with nurses and older siblings. Scanning for

Ky's head, I find him, one hand flung carelessly across Tutan's leg, both boys off content in the land of dreams. My breath comes easier and I watch him sleep for a moment, warm and safe. A baby cries, startling awake its mother who sleepily shushes it, bringing the small child close to her chest for a feeding.

Ky stirs and rolls over, eyes flickering, then opening. I am not the only one who has learned to sleep lightly. Brown eyes find mine and he blinks dreamily, starting to get up. I shake my head and bring a finger to my lips in a quieting motion, then bring my palms together and to the side of my tilted head, indicating he should go back to sleep. Obliging, he rolls over, pulling the blanket over him and his friend. Anubis licks my hand then goes to lie beside his master, body pressed against the small back. Reassured of my brother's well-being, I retreat into the hallway, contemplating where my best chances of finding something to eat lie. I could go to the kitchens to see about begging for some scraps, but want to be alone to think more about Pharaoh and Wujat's words. Remembering the central courtyard in the palace, resplendent with date palms, I try to recall how best to reach the inner gardens, and I start out in their direction.

The silence of the palace feels thick somehow, an invisible weight pressing in from all sides, making me wish for the solid presence of Anubis. Passing another statue, I feel its eyes follow me down the hall, boring into my back. It takes all my resolve not to run. Even so, my pace quickens and after a few wrong turns, where I thankfully don't bump into anyone or anything, I emerge into the cool night air, gulping down several giant breaths. Here, at the heart of the palace, palm fronds blow to and fro in the inky blackness.

Scaling up one of the trees and reaching for some of the lower-hanging specimens, I manage to pluck a few plump dates then inch back down the rough bark, sitting my bottom firmly on the ground. I rest against the palm and devour the sweet fruits, feeling steadier. Licking sticky fingers and now with a full belly, I think more about the evening's revelations. Famine is not good for political stability, particularly when combined with whispers of war. A seed of fear, which took root on my walk here, sprouts in my stomach alongside the dates. Not wanting to nourish it, I turn again to Pharaoh's comment on my father. What kind of friction was he referring to? Could someone from the temple have been involved in my parents' death? A rival? Not that I am necessarily ruling out Pharaoh's own involvement, but his generosity is well-known and there are those who will always seek favour with the king, hoping to reap the rewards.

I had never known Father to do anything for his own gain, yet his passion and talent for medicine — and perhaps a word from Wujat? — had attracted Pharaoh's eye. And now, with some careful manoeuvring, I also seem to have found favour with the ruler of all the land, personally requested to carry out this task of recovering the missing scroll. A forceful breeze rustles the fronds and I shiver. Father used to say that courting "favour" is like dancing with a lion.

Though worries of war, food shortages, and conspiracy are fertilizer to the sprout of fear, I am surprised to also discover a small bud of elation at the thought of resuming my studies. To immerse myself once again in words and learning, to apprentice and help those who are ill, to answer the calling of my own soul is a gift and one that I know Father would not want me to waste. And then there is Ky; I will need all the knowledge at my disposal to help him. If, as my father hoped, there is something in the scroll that can save him — a procedure, an operation, some type of treatment — it must be found as soon as possible. My shoulders straighten. Despite reservations about Pharaoh and Wujat's motives, which something tells me to remain wary of, at the moment their interests are aligned with mine. And that is enough.

Standing, I inhale the fresh night air and, with a nod at the deity travelling across the sky, address him by name. "Watch over me, Khonsu. Something tells me I am going to require all the help the gods can offer."

NOW, REMEMBER TO BEHAVE at the palace," I instruct my brother after breakfast. "We are here by Pharaoh's good graces and don't want to cause unnecessary trouble."

"Ky is no trouble." Tutan waves his cherubically imperious hand. "If anything, he is not trouble enough!" He nudges my brother conspiratorially, who giggles.

"Don't worry, Sesha, these two have their studies to occupy them," says Harwa, the prince's long-suffering tutor. "There is much history to learn."

"A future king should not have to concern himself with things that happened so long ago," Tutan says, hands on pudgy hips.

"You are wrong, my son." Queen Anat strides over to us, voice commanding, robes swishing. Harwa, Ky, and I bow to the Great Royal Wife. "Part of becoming a great king is having the knowledge of and respect for those who came before you. Harwa is tasked with teaching you about our ways and our gods. You must come to know everything about them, for you will need to know the proper one to invoke at what time, when tasked with running the kingdom."

"Yes, Mother," Tutan mutters, looking at the ground.

The queen turns to me. "Sesha, Pharaoh would like to speak with you. Come." She turns without waiting for my response and I swallow. Ky sends me a nervous look and I attempt a reassuring smile.

"All is well," I whisper, squeezing his hand with a fervent prayer for the gods to protect him, then turn to follow quickly after the queen down the hall. She walks briskly, her thick black hair shining in the sun like polished ebony. Most royal women shave their heads, wearing a variety of wigs; however, Queen Anat's hair is beautiful and I do not blame her for wanting to keep her own. I try not to wonder at the honour of having the Great Royal Wife summon me herself, but I know from hearing Father talk that the queen is very much involved in the day-to-day affairs of running the palace and its politics. It is said her brilliance in such matters surpasses even her beauty, which itself is nothing to blink at. Privately, if I had to choose one, it would be the former attribute. In contrast to the latter, it does not diminish with time but grows ever more powerful. I recall Pharaoh's doting eyes for his queen earlier. Though, I suppose both have their uses. The queen's ever-present handmaidens accompany us, walking as silently as shadows at our sides.

"And how are you feeling this morning, Sesha?" Queen Anat inquires with a glance over her shoulder.

"Very well, my lady."

"I imagine the last month must have been quite … precarious," she says. "However did you manage to survive?"

"By the grace of the gods, I suppose." And by relying on instincts I did not know I possessed. Even now, it is something to shift back into my old manner of being, aligning the Sesha of the past with the new one.

"We had your parents entombed in one of the mastabas," she says, without preamble. "I thought you might like to visit them soon."

I suck in a jagged breath at the thought of them lying in one of the Houses for Eternity. "Thank you, My Queen."

"He was a noble servant to our family," she says. Then, with another glance over her shoulder, "Tell me, Sesha, how did you and Ky escape the fire?"

Abruptly, I stop walking. That night is still unclear in my mind. The smoke and heat from the flames. The confusion. The fear. Shouts from my mother and father. Swallowing, I become aware our small party has halted, waiting for me. "I am not entirely sure, Your Majesty," I say. Ky and I slept on the roof. There was a small opening where the smoke from our hearth would escape.

"Perhaps the gods have clouded your mind to spare you the painful memories." Queen Anat turns and clasps her hands, standing regally before me.

"I remember very little from that night," I admit. Aside from the vivid detail of the men, men bearing a distinct emblem, running from the house as Ky and I sat perched in the thatch of the neighbour's roof, coughing, our clothes smouldering, helpless to save our parents. Blinking, I come back to the hallway. The queen is staring at me. My newfound instincts kick in. "In fact, I remember nothing at all."

"That is probably for the best, my child," she says, not unkindly. And we continue our walk down to the great chambers.

I follow the queen into the main royal chambers, the room awash with morning chatter. Strong smells of perfumes and incense infuse the air, mingling with the voices. Ahmes stands beside Wujat and Pharaoh on the steps leading up to the royal dais. There is a sharp pain in my gut. My father used to stand there, hearing the physical complaints of the courtiers and servants milling below. The men look up as we enter and the queen goes to stand beside her husband. Taking her hand, he smiles and kisses her cheek.

"Thank you, my dear."

I stand there, unsure at my summoning, and look to Ahmes, who is holding an intricately painted box. He gives me a slight bow of acknowledgement.

"Sesha," Pharaoh says. "In honour of the task set before you, I would like to present you with a gift."

Whatever I am expecting, it isn't this. Ahmes presents the box to Pharaoh, who holds it aloft.

"Step forward, my child."

I do as he says, spine straight, eyes locked with his.

"As you begin your studies, I would like to offer this token of our appreciation, in recognition of your quest to seek out the missing scroll. May the gods bless these instruments and may they serve you well." A shaft of light shines in from the window and hits the rectangular box, illuminating the elaborate designs painted on the wood. I step forward to receive the gift, noting with a sort of detached clarity as my hands reach up that my nails are still ragged and torn and there is grime under the left thumb that I have been unable to scrub away. If Pharaoh notices, he gives no sign, and I bow low, taking the box from his outstretched hands.

"Thank you, My King. I am overwhelmed by the honour." And I am. Looking down at the familiarly shaped palette in my hands, I know what it will contain. The tools of a scribe.

"Open it," Pharaoh says.

I oblige, lifting the wooden lid off, breath catching at the beauty of the instruments within. The reeds, polished to a flawless finish, slim and smooth, beckon my fingers to free them from their beds; the brushes perfectly frayed at their tips, ready to swirl through the rich red and inky black minerals packed firm into two depressions in the palette. A delicate roll of blank papyrus lays nestled on the other side of the reeds; expensive and time-consuming to make, this will be saved for recording something special.

I have yet to speak, so engrossed am I in the details of the gift, and I become aware of Wujat clearing his throat in an attempt to hasten my response.

"Forgive me, Your Highness," I stammer. "Your generosity seems to have caused my words to flee."

"Let us hope these tools help you recapture them permanently," Pharaoh says in a hearty voice.

I bow low again and the queen gives a commanding clap. She puts her hand on Pharaoh's offered arm and the pair turn and walk up to take their seats as the talking and music resume. Wujat and Ahmes come to my side.

"I will accompany you to the temple, Sesha," Wujat says. "There are a few last-minute instructions Pharaoh wishes me to impart." He turns and walks out the door, white robes swishing. I follow, box clutched tightly under my arm. It, more than anything, reminds me of who I used to be. Of who I still can be.

"May the gods be with you," Ahmes calls behind me. Glancing over my shoulder at his face, I am taken aback by the expression in his eyes. I hope whatever is concerning Ahmes has naught to do with me. Yet, something tickling against the nape of my neck whispers this is not so.

10

"**S**ESHA, HOW OFTEN DID you frequent the temple with your father?" Wujat asks, striding down the sandy path in front of me.

"Often, Your Holiness." I had accompanied my father to temple since before my two feet touched the earth.

"You are aware of what classes will be like, yes?" We walk by the women grinding grain for the palace. Their chatter and laughter fills the air, mixing with the citrusy sweet smell of lemongrass tea being brewed in the neighbouring huts.

"I know they are very intensive," I say, suddenly nervous. Students study the hieratic script for years, working toward mastering thousands of complex hieroglyphs and reproducing them precisely. Thanks to my father's teachings, which began officially in my third year, I am familiar with most of the general symbols. It is the specific medical terminology I will need to become more familiar with. Not only to become a physician, but also to transcribe the missing surgical scroll as accurately as possible.

If I can find it, that is.

"Yes," Wujat says, interrupting my thoughts. "Quite intensive. Though from what your father said, I understand you are an excellent student and quite proficient with the glyphs. You will be joining the advanced medical class at the temple." He casts me a sidelong look. "And will be the only girl, of course."

Advanced students were in their final year, divided into their respective concentrations. Temple scribes, those who would reside at the palace, census takers, collectors of taxes, recorders of business transactions, and, of course, the medical scribes, many of whom would go on to become doctors and then go out to the communities up and down the Nile and even farther beyond. It is known throughout the lands that the best doctors are trained right here in Thebes.

"The discipline is often harsh," Wujat continues. Scribes are often struck if they are unable to exactly replicate the intricate hieroglyphs, or too slow in their work. Perhaps that is why our word for "teach," *seba*, also means "to beat." "Your teachers won't be easy on you because you are female, or because of who your father was. The expectations will be higher, in fact."

"By Amun's grace, may I live up to them," I say, not at all sure of my abilities, but not wanting to give Wujat cause to doubt my finding the scroll.

"From what your father told me, I am sure you will." A smile relaxes his normally austere face as we round a curve in the path. "He was very proud of you, Sesha."

I manage a small nod, throat tight.

Clearing it, I hazard a question to Wujat. "You mentioned the priest that shared the scroll with my father recently passed on. What happened to him?"

"Qar?" Wujat furrows his brow. "Yes, he fell ill not long after your father's … accident. Most sudden. It's been a tumultuous month at the temple."

The building in question looms into view, as big as the palace and equally resplendent. A thrill runs through me at the sight of it. The enormous structure seems to pulse with a life of its own, the heart of the city. And despite the critical task set before me, I cannot help but feel exhilarated to be back in this place, to finish the training that my father started.

But first.

The marketplace spreads out in all directions, like tributaries of the giant river it sits beside. Tents of all different colours — several tattered, many wind-beaten, most fraying around the edges — flutter side by side as merchants and vendors shout to ensnare the attention of anyone walking by. My shoulders automatically hunch and my eyes go to the sandy earth, hoping a good wash and Nebet's work is enough to disguise me from the always-vigilant eyes of the hawkers.

I know every one of them — which ones to watch out for, ready with their sharp sticks to smack away errant hands, which ones will leave scraps from the day for those who do not have enough to eat. The fruit stand is just ahead, six rows up, three stalls off to the right. Close enough to the path, where I will be visible.

Feigning interest in the grain items at a table just up and over to the left, I step quickly behind Wujat; his lean frame is at least better than nothing, cover-wise. He stops, waiting patiently for me to complete my fake perusing of the stall's goods. Lucky for me, its vendor, one of the kinder ones, is currently haggling with her neighbour about how many onions are equal to five loaves of bread.

As their negotiations come to a close, I steel myself and turn to follow Wujat up the path with a demure smile and apologetic nod at my stomach. Four rows to go.

Three.

Two.

One.

Already I've picked out the nasal tones of the vendor's wife, high-pitched and as prickly as the desert plant that grows to the south. My shoulders hunch even higher, and I walk on Wujat's left, trying to stay perfectly in line with his frame. People are aware of him as we pass, and they bow deferentially. The bolder ones vie for his attention, calling out specials reserved only for the esteemed vizier, the fat fruit vendor unfortunately being among them.

"Bring the gods fresh honourings, Your Holiness!" my foul-breathed, would-be assassin cries.

"Not today." Wujat does not turn his head.

I follow suit, ducking my head lower, not daring to glance even the tiniest sliver to my right. The vendor mutters something under his breath and I hear him continue on in his assault of other customers, wielding his vicious halitosis at liberty.

At last we reach the opening of the temple and my shoulders relax a royal cubit. The air already feels cooler, whisping out of the shade from within the stone walls. Colossal statues guard the entrance and tall, wide pillars reach the sky, inscribed with beautiful artwork and intricate texts.

Wujat removes his fine leather shoes and steps into the small footbath provided at the entrance, washing his soles in purification. I step into another bath, grabbing the pumice beside it, and scrub away at the dirt. At last, feet cleaned, bodies purified by the smoking myrrh waved over us by junior priests, we bow to the golden bust of Osiris and enter the inner recesses of the temple. More towering columns line the hallways, circular and massive; several paths lead off in different directions.

My flesh prickles; the scroll is hidden here somewhere, I can feel it. Like last night in the palace, it takes all my restraint not to run through the temple, not in fear this time, but in a frenzied hunt for the document. We walk down the path to our left and end up in an enormous room, a circular maze with concentric waist-high walls, rings that decrease in circumference as they lead into the centre where a large flood of light streams in through the triangular opening at the top of the temple. It brightens the whole space, bouncing off strategically placed copper mirrors, illuminating all corners of the room.

"May the gods of good fortune be with you, Sesha," Wujat murmurs as an officiant wearing a gleaming gold necklace strides over. I recognize him as the High Priest who succeeded my father, who had succeeded Wujat himself. "And remember, complete discretion is probably best with regards to your … inquiry."

"Your Holiness." The officiant bows as he approaches. His nose is large, perhaps in an attempt to remain in proportion with his giant head, which bears a large brown mark exposed by his lack of hair, all of it having been plucked from his body, as is the custom.

"Nebifu," Wujat says, nodding. "How are things, here?"

"All is well. To what do we owe such an honour as to have the Great Wujat visit us himself so frequently this moon?" Nebifu lifts an invisible brow. There is something in the tilt of his chin, not quite impertinence, but something …

"I bring you a new student, final year." Wujat nods at me.

"Classes are full." Nebifu barely spares me a glance down his mammoth proboscis. Perhaps there is a tumour in there somewhere. "Besides, we are halfway through the session. He will be behind. Wait until the harvest season, when we begin anew."

"*She* will start now," Wujat says, voice firm. "I think you know Sesha, Daughter of Ay, Great Healer of the Land and former Chief Scribe and Priest."

Nebifu bristles, recognition laced with disdain. "A girl?"

"Does that matter?" I finally find my voice. Though the feminine is typically embraced and celebrated in our culture, there are some who hold it in contempt. Father never liked Nebifu, and I suppose his distaste for the man has rubbed off on me, though he was never overt about his criticisms.

Nebifu glares at me and I lower my eyes; my outburst is severely out of turn. Whip worthy, in fact.

Wujat attempts to smooth the tension. "I am sure you will find Sesha quite a diligent student. From what I hear, the girl is already an exceptional healer."

Nebifu harrumphs. "No special treatment will be given. If her knowledge is insufficient, her teachers will let me know. We do not have space for those who are unable to keep up."

Clutching my writing instruments close to my chest prevents me from dropping them onto the ground, my hands from curling into small, but surprisingly accurate, fists. If I were a boy, you can be sure special treatment would indeed be given.

I open my mouth, which has been functioning more and more of late with a will of its own.

Wujat sends me a sharp look, effectively binding the words about to break free. "Perfectly understandable." He turns to me, gesturing to a narrow lane leading through the concentric circles into the centre of the temple. Other junior scribes sit cross-legged around their teacher, who is etching out hieroglyphs on the dusty floor. "Go on then, Sesha. Join your classmates."

Gulping down deep breaths of myrrh-saturated air, I walk toward the group basked in Ra's light, blinking my eyes to adjust to the increasing brightness. As I near them, several faces turn to look at me, expressions ranging from open curiosity to deep suspicion, causing my stomach to curl in on itself.

And just like that, here I go.

11

"WHO HERE CAN TELL ME THE proper treatment for involuntary loosening of the bowels?" the scribe asks, voice commanding.

"The gum of the acacia tree," I blurt automatically, then blush. Nobody likes an outsider with all the answers. But it is too late. The scribe turns to me and the remaining heads that have not swivelled at my approach do so now.

"Can you explain in what way?" the scribe says. With his bald head, he looks similar to Nebifu, though he lacks the birthmark and his nose is not quite as offensive. He is also much heavier. Evidently he likes to help the gods consume any leftover food offerings.

"It is, uh, often mixed with bubbling water to form a thick solution and acts as a soothing coating to the insides when swallowed." I try my best not to stammer.

"What are its other uses?" he demands, round cheeks puffing out.

"Treatment for bleeding gums and other oral disorders, maladies of the throat, open wounds, eye sores, and a salve for lesions in and around a person's, um, anus, Sebau." I use our formal address for teacher.

He turns at the snickers, eyes homing in on a tall student with hair a few shades darker than the wheat in the fields. "Is there anything you can add to this, Paser?"

The boy he addresses straightens, eyes going from his clay tablet to the scribe. "Yes. These lesions can be most uncomfortable, Sebau." He scratches his backside for emphasis. The other students laugh and the scribe's sigh is forceful enough to huff out a torch.

"Take your food now," he says and the boys scatter. He turns to me. Briefly, I wish for the quiet authority of Wujat over my shoulder. "What is your name?"

"Sesha." I leave out my formal title. He will find out who my father is soon enough.

He peers closely at me. "I recognize you. Ay's daughter."

I acknowledge this with a small nod. Sooner than I thought.

"Tell me, Daughter of Ay, are you also aware of the proper incantation to go with the administering of the acacia?"

"It depends on the reason for which it is being administered."

"Let us assume it is an oral malady."

"An ailment with which one shall contend?"

"Yes, yes." He is impatient. Everyone knows the incantations for an ailment not to be treated: a blessing for the patient to go as quickly and painlessly as possible to the afterlife. Which, unfortunately, is a real possibility with oral cases, especially if one does not use their chewing stick at least twice a day.

I am about to deliver what I am fairly sure is the correct incantation when the tall student walks over to us.

"There is another dead rat in the ale vat, Sebau," he calls out as if this is an everyday occurrence. Maybe it is; the temple has its own brewery and likely more than a few rats lurking in the deep and dark recesses underground.

The scribe turns to him. "So fish it out."

"Reb tried to, but …" Paser pauses. His eyes are a rich brown, like the fertile soil of the riverbanks after the floods.

"But?" the scribe prompts.

"He fell in."

"The boy can swim, can't he? A dead rat in the beer is one thing …"

"It is only that he swallowed a large quantity of the brew while calling for help, and seems quite intoxicated, Sebau."

The scribe throws his hands up. "Imbeciles." He storms off in the direction of the other boys, muttering to himself about them being no smarter than the rodents. Glancing around, I wonder if anyone will notice if I sneak off to Father's old study. I've concluded this is the most logical place to begin my search. Then again Wujat *had* mentioned discretion.

Paser looks at me and holds out a mug of the nutritious drink.

"No, thank you."

He shrugs and takes a long guzzle, wiping his mouth with the back of his hand when he finishes. My throat swallows involuntarily. "There was no rat, in case that changes your mind." He holds out the drink again.

I don't mention that I've actually eaten rats for breakfast, and they are not so terrible when well cooked, but instead accept the beverage. It is cold and aside from the odd lump, very refreshing. I pass it back to Paser.

"Reb just wanted a little extra refreshment, though he'll be black and blue tomorrow for that stunt."

"Why did you tell Sebau?"

"Better for Reb if he deals with it and not his uncle."

"His uncle?"

He nods at High Priest Nebifu, at the outer edge of the concentric circles, still talking to Wujat, the pair deep in serious conversation.

"He would be severely … punished for bringing shame to his family."

"Then why take the risk?"

Paser looks at me. "You've never taken a risk before?"

"I have." This is an understatement.

"Then you must know that sometimes people do things that contradict reason. Especially when it is hot. And when lessons are long and tedious. And when the beer tastes good." He takes another long drink then offers the mug again. I shake my head.

"It is nice to hear that my classmates take their studies so seriously."

"Reb takes it seriously enough." He looks at me with a conceding grin. "Though he is perhaps a little impulsive."

"What of his father?" The scribe position is generally kept in families, passing from father to son.

"Dead, as is mine." So we have something else in common besides risk-taking. Queen Anat had said my parents lie in one of the mastabas. Suddenly, a tide of intense longing sucks at my spirit, a need to see them.

"Do you know where Pharaoh's physician and his wife rest?" I ask Paser abruptly. My father was highly regarded in the kingdom. Even the scribes-in-training would be aware of the place his remains lie. What is left of them.

Paser's eyes flicker over me. "Ah, yes, of course. You are the daughter of Ay, Chief ..."

"My name is Sesha." I cut him off before he goes into the full pronouncement of his title.

A few of the other boys have come back, the excitement from the beer-vat incident having calmed somewhat. Reb is among them, his ears bright red, most likely from being freshly boxed. A trickle of blood runs down the left one and drips from his lobe like a melting garnet earring. His tunic is soaked through.

"It is a wonder they let your parents be buried with any ceremony at all," he hiccups, ears and wet clothes seemingly giving him no concern.

I whirl on him. "What do you mean?" My voice is sharp.

"Your father —" Reb starts, rubbing at an older welt on his upper right arm. Perhaps a result of not knowing the proper incantation.

"Was much respected," Paser interrupts.

Several sharp claps have the boys skittering back to their places. Sebau strides over, looking distinctly put out and dripping slightly. The smell of yeast is strong in the air.

"Now, if everyone is feeling properly refreshed," Sebau begins, "let us get back to our lessons. Daughter of Ay, take your place there." He points to an empty reed mat. Obediently, I go and sit, clutching my precious tools. Included are some pieces of limestone with which to practise my scripts. Carefully, I remove the elegant reeds from their inlaid case.

Paser leans over my shoulder and whistles softly. "Some beautiful supplies you have there."

"It was a gift."

Or a bribe. I am not sure which.

"No talking!" Sebau smacks a long knobbed stick with wicked-looking flays at the end onto the ground, sending a spray of dust in the air. It appears a trip to Father's study will not be happening in the next little while.

Looking down at the shards of limestone, I am careful not to speak for the rest of class, as we practise inscribing the cursive hieratic script for what feels like eternity. While we work, I begin to formulate a plan. Wujat said the temple was searched but I don't have much faith in illiterate guards. Especially ones who may have had something to do with my parents' death. And my father wouldn't leave something so valuable lying out in the open. There is a good chance the scroll is hidden somewhere in his old chambers … which would be Nebifu's now. Reb's uncle. I dart a look at the unfriendly boy, then at the strict Sebau. I need to figure out a way get into that study.

Blinking, I look up from my tablet only as the light begins to fade. My fingers are cramped and blistered, having not been used in this manner for so long. Yet my heart has been somewhat soothed by the meditative act of drawing out the complex symbols, my focus so complete it momentarily forgot the things that trouble it. However, these quickly return as I pack up my tools with the other students. Most will not even look at me; those who do, do so in obvious derision. Paser being the exception.

"You have a fair hand," he says to me. "See you tomorrow."

So taken aback by his compliment, I say nothing, watching as he walks away with a few of the other boys, leaning over to sniff Reb. He says something and the others erupt into laughter.

"Sesha." I look up. Ky is there with Anubis. "We have come to walk you home." His head has been closely shorn, most likely to rid him of the lice, especially as he is in close proximity to the royal children.

My loneliness evaporates some.

"Thank you, Brother," I say, walking over to him and brushing my hand across his cropped head, feeling the soft prickling of his hair against my palm. "They did not take it all the way to the scalp?" To a trained eye the swelling is more apparent, skin taut against the skull.

"It is the latest fashion for the older children at court," he says, ducking out from under my hand.

"Perhaps I should cut mine." My fingertips brush back my own hair, which I have become rather attached to. I braided it this morning to keep it out of my way but a few strands have managed to escape.

"You are a scribe, now," Ky teases as we walk out of the temple, Anubis at our side. Ra is low on the horizon and the vendors of the marketplace have gone home for their suppers. "You no longer need to concern yourself with being fashionable."

I let out a half snort, looks having been the least of my concerns this past month. Battling constant filth, grit, and sand fleas had made up the bulk of my hygiene routine.

"Were you able to find out anything about the scroll?" Ky asks.

"No," I admit. "The teachers watch us like the falcon watches her prey. Though it appears more was going on with Father than we know of."

"Like what?" Ky asks, one hand on Anubis's head.

"I am not sure, exactly." I think of Pharaoh and Wujat's late-night conversation; even Ahmes and Reb had alluded to something, though both were vague. "But there is something in the way people speak his name." With an inflection I cannot quite decipher. Casting a look at the emptying room, I lower my voice. "I plan to search his old chambers, perhaps the scroll is hidden there somewhere. What about you? Were you able to find anything out?"

"Nothing of the scroll. I did learn where Mother and Father are being kept." His voice is soft but it stops me mid-step.

I swallow. "Me, too."

He looks up at me. "Will you go to see them?"

"I wanted to wait for you." We could go now, but neither of us mentions it. I wonder if our hesitation has something to do with the uncertainty of their fate. When we die our soul splits into two parts: the *Ka*, our unique life force, flies off to enjoy the afterlife, while the *Ba*, our individual personality, keeps watch over our families. Each night they return to the tomb to join back together, resting and recharging before doing it all again the next day. This is why we go to so much trouble to preserve the bodies. The *Ba* and *Ka* need the physical body, the *Akh*, to house the soul. If my parents' remains are ... unrecognizable, will the *Ka* and *Ba* be able to reunite or find their way home? And if not, will they vanish forever, unable to watch over us or reach paradise?

"Tell me of your day," I say to distract us both as we leave the temple. "What of the gossip at the palace?"

He perks up. "Well, one of the lesser wives screamed at the cook for burning her food and said she was trying to poison her. And Merat was arguing with Queen Anat about something, a suitor she was finding most disagreeable. It seems he has a habit of spitting when he talks ..." Ky chatters on about the minor trials and tribulations of palace life as we continue our walk; Anubis trotting at our left, Ra on our right, winking good night before disappearing below the horizon. Half of my mind pays attention to Ky while the other half, wanting to avoid further agonizing over the state of my parents' souls, attempts to devise a way to sneak into Nebifu's chambers undetected. Will I need to befriend the hideous Reb? I cannot just wish for the scroll to reveal itself without any real effort on my behalf. If my hunch is wrong and it is not there, I will have to systematically search the sprawling temple, which, along with the surrounding buildings and underground catacombs, is vast and ancient. And though I have been praying to the gods to aid me in my task, as I learned from my father, it is best if one does not leave everything entirely up to them.

12

BACK AT THE PALACE, I see Ky safely off with Tutan and return to the handmaidens' chambers. Dinner has been served and I help myself to the leftover food at the table near the front of the room. It is mostly fruit and some dry bread but still a thousand times more delicious than anything I ate before returning to the palace.

Bebi flits over to my side, head cocked, eyes bright. "One of the cooks was let go today. It is said she was trying to poison a wife of Pharaoh."

"What would be her reason for doing so?" I say, reminding myself to first chew, then swallow.

"Who knows?" She shrugs. "Perhaps she was envious?"

"The cook?" Despite it being a great honour to serve the pharaoh and his family, I can see how toiling for people who do not always appreciate their riches might be trying.

"No, the wife." Bebi grins. "The cook is young and quite beautiful."

"Which wife was it?" I ask, not having gleaned that particular detail from Ky.

"Senseneb."

"Ah." One of Pharaoh's newer and younger queens, she is reputed to be quite vain, with a violent temper. I dimly recall talk of her and Queen Anat having some heated confrontations when the princess first moved into the palace. However, the Great Royal Wife is most respected and revered among the court, the public, and, of course, Pharaoh himself. Senseneb must have seen how it is and, apparently, not being entirely stupid, taken her frustrations out on someone else. It is fortunate the girl escaped with only the loss of her duties and nothing else. She must be a very good cook.

"How was your day?" Bebi asks me, curious. "It is not most tedious in the temple for hours on end?"

"No, it is quite wonderful. I learned four new glyphs today, intricate ones," I say, and am shocked at the satisfaction in my voice. Guilt immediately overwhelms me at the less satisfactory progress I've made in my secret assignment. However, I suppose one gets one's bearings before charting a course. At least tomorrow I have a specific goal: to get into Nebifu's quarters. Unobserved.

"Sesha," a commanding voice says. I turn and face Merat.

Her pretty face is still imposing and her arms are crossed over one another. She walks up to me, handmaidens bobbing deferentially at her approach.

"Yes, Princess?" I bow, as does Bebi.

She lowers her voice. "I wish to begin our lessons. Now."

Despite my exhaustion, I force myself to smile. "Of course, Princess. Do you have a specific location in mind for your schooling?"

"My chambers." She turns without waiting for my response and I follow her out of the room. I see Kewat look at me, eyes narrowed, and whisper something to the girl standing beside her, who clasps a hand to her mouth to keep a giggle from escaping.

"You may walk beside me, Sesha," the princess says as we leave the handmaidens' quarters, and I obey, falling into step at her side.

"How were your lessons today?"

"I am behind with some of the glyphs," I admit, while wondering at the princess's interest. Is she meant to be keeping an eye on me for someone? I sense no deception in her demeanour but keep the conversation away from today's failed search all the same.

"I am sure it will come back to you," she says. "I saw you there when I went to temple this morning to bring the gods offerings on little Tabira's behalf."

"How is she doing?" I ask.

"Better. Though when The Fever comes on she says it feels like her bones are breaking apart in her skin."

"It will return intermittently, then?"

"That is what Ahmes says."

"There is a tea that may treat some of her symptoms." I wonder if Ahmes is familiar with it. My mother used to make it for my father, who dispensed it freely to his patients. She often prepared his medicines, in addition to sought-after perfumes and creams for the court. "I can brew her some."

"Thank you," she says, tone softening a shade. "And how are your classmates?"

"Nothing I cannot bear," I say, thinking of some of the unpleasant characters I have had to deal with of late.

"They do not mind having a female in their midst?"

"Some may," I say. "Though one boy was civil at least."

"Yes, I saw you speaking with him. What is his name?"

There is a subtle shift in her tone. I glance at her but she keeps looking straight ahead.

"Paser."

"I thought so," she murmurs, almost to herself.

"Does Your Highness know him?"

"We played together as children," she says. "His grandfather was a high-ranking general who often held council with Father and Wujat."

"Would you like me to bring him a greeting?"

"No." Her tone is clipped. "That is not necessary."

I refrain from saying anything more on the subject as we arrive at her chambers. So it is not only me that piques her interest, but also a boy. I feel abashed at my mistrust, as well as a pang for the loss of my innocence, carried away on the wind, along with my parents' ashes. Merat nods at the guard standing outside her door, who bows and moves aside to let us in.

Her room, or rooms, rather, are resplendent. Gold glints from every surface in the setting sun. There is a large bed in the centre, a sprawling confection of fine linens embroidered in rich emerald and azure hues, gauzy netting draped from the beams surrounding it. The windows are larger and lower than typical, also with netting, and face east to allow maximum viewing of the sunrise. She has her own private bath with large mirrors extending down one side of the room. There are some cushions in a pile by one of the windows. I notice she has assembled some bits of broken pottery called ostraca and some writing materials. A few scrolls lie scattered on the floor beside the cushions.

"Where did you get these?" I ask, walking over. Unable to resist, I pick one up, feeling its lovely texture with my fingertips.

"Do you like them?" she asks, avoiding my question.

I unwind one of the long leather strings from around the scroll and unroll it. The sheet of papyrus crackles under my fingertips and the intoxicating scent of pulped reed permeates the air.

"Yes," is all I can manage.

"Consider them your payment, then, for my lessons." She waves a careless hand.

Carefully, I roll up the document. "I cannot accept, Your Highness." Though none appear to be the one I seek, they look to be sacred texts. "It is too much. Besides, a princess should not have to pay for her lessons."

"Do you not consider that a great irony?" she says. "That those who have the most receive all things for free, expected to pay for nothing?"

Briefly, I wonder if she is testing me somehow. This is unusual thinking for a princess, for any member of nobility for that matter. Ashamedly, until I was forced to scratch out an existence for my brother and myself, the notion never occurred to me. Thanks to Father's respected position, we enjoyed a most comfortable life before that night. And though I am blessed that my fortunes have again changed with the winds, this time I will not be so blind to the injustices I witnessed while trying to survive.

"Where would you like to begin?" Pretending not to hear her question, I set the scroll down. "With your studies? Do you have any schooling at all?"

"I did not pay much attention to my teachings," she admits, "but I know some basic glyphs."

"That is a start." There are over seven hundred of them. "Any hieratic?" This is the cursive script that allows one to write quickly, without needing to etch out the time-consuming hieroglyphs.

"No."

"If I may ask, Your Majesty, why do you wish to read and write? This will help me to direct your studies."

"It is a useful skill," she says. "Many royal women are well versed in *mdju netjer*, the words of the gods."

"And?" I prompt, sensing more.

She shrugs and turns to one of the windows. "I have words inside me that I wish to record. So many that if I do not get them down, I fear they will be lost forever."

"Your Highness is a poet?" I try not to smile.

"Something of the sort."

"Then we will start with some basic hieratic scripts," I say, picking up one of the reed brushes. "Now, if Your Majesty will take a seat?"

I RETURN TO THE HANDMAIDENS' chambers, exhausted, but satisfied at how the lesson went. Merat is a quick learner with a good hand, and she dropped some of her cool reserve as the lesson went on. Despite my protests, she made me take one of the priceless scrolls with me, amplifying my guilt at suspecting her motivations. After a month of trusting no one but Ky, it is a difficult habit to shake, and one I'm not sure I should.

The room is dark, though a slice of moonlight shines in through the windows. I make my way to my bed, slipping the scroll into the box at the head of my mat, meant for each maiden's personal possessions. It is the lone item. Bebi, like everyone else, is sleeping, soft snores escaping with each breath.

I go to wash, pouring water from one of the earthen jugs onto a piece of linen and scrubbing my face. On the way back to my mat a muffled noise comes from off to my left. I recognize the sound, having made it often this past month: the choking back of sobs, meant for no one's ears.

I hesitate at the bed. "Are you you all right?" I say softly.

The girl sits up, baleful black eyes peering at me under messy hair and flushed cheeks. "Go away, Weasel." It is Kewat, the older girl whose disdain for me yesterday was palpable. It is no less so this evening.

I stiffen. "My apologies, I only thought that you were ill."

"Something I ate," she mutters, brushing a piece of hair back from her face.

"Ask one of the cooks to prepare you an infusion of mint and ginger in warm water. It has a calming effect on indigestion."

She snorts scornfully and I continue walking to my bed, momentarily regretting not giving her the recipe for loosening of the bowels instead.

"Don't mind her, Sesha," Bebi says sleepily, rolling over onto her side. "She has been most ill-humoured of late, since discovering she may be with child."

Surprised, I look back at Kewat but she has rolled over on her side, her back facing me. "Who is the father?"

"I do not know. Nor even if she is, indeed, expecting. However, I do believe she is late in her courses."

"If so, may Bes watch over her and the babe," I murmur, naming a protective god of the family, especially women and children. Climbing under my blanket, I close my eyes, the day's events replaying in my mind: attending temple, strategizing my search, Merat's lesson, Ky's condition … Aware of the building tension that has my teeth clenching and heart pounding, I let my breath come in and out, trying to relax my body piece by piece from toes to scalp.

"Your brother was looking for you," Bebi yawns.

The tension comes creeping back. "Do you know what he wanted? Is he all right?" All seemed well when I saw him earlier.

"He was in great spirits," she reassures me, but there is something in her face …

"And?" I press.

"He wished me to inform you that he has been invited to attend the royal hippo hunt tomorrow with young Prince Tutan."

"What?" I sit upright, fully awake now. "Does he not realize how dangerous that is?"

"I believe that, in part, was the reason for his excitement." She tries to keep the laughter from bubbling over. "It is a right of passage for the prince," she chides gently. *And a great honour for Ky to be invited along.* The words go unspoken, but I know Ky should not refuse even if he wants to, which clearly he does not.

"Good night, Sesha." Bebi rolls over and, unburdened of her message, promptly falls asleep.

Fretting under my blanket, I cast dark looks at Bebi's slumbering form. Easy for her to remain untroubled —

Ky is not her brother. Hunting hippos is fraught with peril. I have seen its effects up close, helping Father stitch gaping wounds or amputate limbs crushed by the stampeding animals. It is not uncommon for several men from each hunt to suffer such horrible injuries, or worse. My one hope is that Pharaoh will not let the young boys get too close until that last moment when Tutan delivers the mortal wound to the beast, taking one step closer to becoming a man.

I need to be on that hunt. If something happens to Ky then I can be close at hand. Ahmes must be going. I wonder if there is any way I can convince him to let me join. The hunt will most likely take place at dusk tomorrow when the hippo is most active, thus adding to the sport. Tossing, I turn over, facing in the direction of Kewat. The sounds coming from her cot have subsided.

On top of everything else I still have not worked out a way to get into Nebifu's chambers. Sighing, I resign myself to very little sleep this night.

I am distracted all that morning in my studies, unable to focus on the lesser-known hieroglyphs needed to understand complicated medical procedures nor on my plan to sneak into my father's old study. No matter, I think grimly, Ky will not need the surgery if he is trampled by a hippo first. Paser mentions that Ahmes is teaching us after our midday meal.

"Would it not be nice to eat as the pharaoh does?" Reb lifts a stale piece of bread off his plate in disgust and throws it on the ground. Decent food is provided for the scribes, but the junior ones are often left the scraps of their seniors. Still not quite accustomed to knowing where my next meal is coming from, I barely resist the urge to pounce on the dry roll.

"But then you would have to sit around all day, listening to people drone on about nothing but trivial matters such as the latest trends at court and who wore the same wig twice in a row." Paser rolls his eyes.

"I would not mind," Reb mutters. "It would be a welcome change. Not to mention all that power they have." His voice is filled with longing. "And to be remembered, when I have passed into the afterlife." There is a large fresh bruise high on his cheekbone and surrounding one eye. Perhaps his uncle heard about the beer-vat incident after all.

"And who do you think has the power to choose what is remembered among those who come after us?" Paser says, picking the seeds out of his melon. "We do."

"I think the pyramids will also do a decent job of that," I add.

He turns to me, gaze intense. "But who inscribes the stories on their walls? Who writes of the great queens and kings on their tombs and monuments? Who keeps records, receipts of the entire kingdom and decides what information is passed on and what is not?" Paser gestures at us. "Scribes. Our words have power."

I can see why Merat is intrigued by Paser. He has a most compelling manner, not to mention the added bonus of not spitting when he talks. I can also see why she did not want me to bring him a message. His disdain for palace life, and presumably its occupants, is apparent.

A loud gong interrupts Paser's impassioned speech. We turn our heads at Ahmes's approach. He is followed by two other scribes carrying supplies. He seems different here in the temple, taller, his authority even stronger somehow. I smile at him but he takes no special note of me.

"Today we will be discussing the preparation and use of sutures on open wounds," he says by way of opening, putting the instruments down. One of the scribes places a large bowl of sheep intestines on the ground. Fresh ones. A few bloated flies drift lazily up from the lumpy mess they've been sampling.

"I will demonstrate how to properly cut the intestines and then you will take over. A few of you will assist in cutting up linen bandages." The other scribe places a heap of clean cloths on the mat in front of Ahmes.

Knowing what I do of the hunt today, this seems a timely subject.

"Do I have volunteers for the sutures?" Most of the hands shoot up, including mine. I have my own reasons for wanting to make sure that they are of the highest quality.

An hour later I am happily up to my elbows in still-warm sheep guts, a pile of sinewy thread on my right.

"Though we mostly use linen and other plant fibres for stitching, the benefit of using the animal sinew is there is no need to remove the sutures, as they dissolve on their own," Ahmes is saying. He describes the different types of stitches — continuous, interrupted — and the virtue of each. There is a pile of hides that we can take our turn practising on. "It is important to make sure the wound is free from foreign objects and that the bleeding is not excessive." He picks up a needle and demonstrates the proper way of threading it, licking one end of the fresh intestinal string.

I make my way over, hoping to find a moment to ask whether I might accompany him on this evening's festivities. He passes the threaded needle to Reb, who enthusiastically jams it in and out of a hide. I feel a brief spurt of pity for his potential patients.

Seizing my chance, I take a deep breath. Ahmes has been kind but that does not mean he will be open to my suggestion.

"I have heard you will be in attendance at this evening's hunt," I begin.

"No," he says, frowning slightly, without looking up from Reb's handiwork. "Less force, boy."

"You are not going?" I look up at him.

He glances at me then, brown eyes stern, but there is a flash of amusement in them. "I am. You, however, are not."

"But you may need my help."

"I have help." He nods at the two scribes who brought the items over, both looking smug at their duties.

"But if anything happens to my brother …"

"It will cause you to lose your medical detachment, thus rendering you useless," he finishes. His tone softens. "I am most fond of Ky, Sesha. Trust that I will see him safe."

"I do, but —"

"That is all." He turns away from me and addresses the class. "Clean up your areas. We are finished for today."

Everyone scrambles to clear away the mess. Grumbling to myself, I try to come up with another way to join the expedition, storing my precious tools under my reed mat, as the others do, ready for tomorrow's work.

"What were you asking of Ahmes?" Paser asks, striding over, his hair catching the last few glints of the sun.

Sighing, I flick a piece of sheep offal from my robe. "I wished to accompany him on the hippo hunt this eve, but he denied my request."

"You think you should be assisting him?" Reb overhears, incredulous. "It is your second day and you presume to accompany the pharaoh's physician on a most holy and sacred duty? Your pride is something to behold, Sesha, as your father's was before you."

This is the second time he has mentioned my father and I will not let it go unaddressed.

"If you have something to say about my father, then out with it." My fists curl up at my side. Reb is much bigger, but I am agile and strike quickly. Apep taught me that much.

He takes another step toward me as the other boys gather round, forming a tight circle around us.

14

"**W**HAT OF MY FATHER?**"** I repeat through gritted teeth. If there are words being said about him, I wish to know.

"It is said that he offended the gods," he sneers. "That is why he was killed."

I step back as if Reb has physically struck me.

"And how did he do this?" My father always offered proper tribute. But Reb's words shake loose a memory, a few evenings just before his death.

Father's instruments are laid out on the wooden table, gleaming in the sun while he inspects them, as he does most nights before a surgery. The last few weeks have been very busy with the Inundation now upon us. It is Akhet, the season when the Nile's waters flood the riverbanks, leaving behind fertile black earth for the crops to be planted in, giving fresh food and new life to the kingdom. Since the farmers are free during this time they come in from the submerged fields, honoured to serve the pharaoh by providing the much-needed labour for the annual repairs to the pyramids and temples of the region.

This means Father and the physicians under him are besieged by accidental injuries: broken bones from falling slabs of rock, cuts, scrapes, and bruises from heaving equipment, and all of the general commotion that comes with an active site of construction. Father technically isn't really supposed to tend to the workers, his duty being first and foremost to the royal family and members of the court, but he is fascinated by the unique injuries that accompany the Inundation, always seizing the opportunity to learn more. He managed to convince Wujat to let him tend to some of the more serious cases, though the lesser medical scribes were responsible for the bulk of the patients.

I watch his hand, fine-boned, yet strong and capable, as he checks each of his tools — forceps, clamps, tinuculum — making sure all are in working order. His fingers stop at his most prized blade, a black one composed of a rare volcanic glass called obsidian. My mother had found it at the market, brought in by a ship sailing from a distant land. She gave it to Father as a wedding gift. He runs his finger along the razor-sharp utensil and a thin line of blood wells.

"This one never dulls," he says, looking up at me, a wide grin on his handsome face. Father's teeth are still very good for his age, due to his dutiful brushing and rinsing after eating. He always says it is all the sand in our food that eventually grinds our teeth away.

"Do you think you will save many lives tomorrow, Baba?" I ask, legs swinging from the rough bench I sit upon.

"If the gods are with me, Sesha," my father says.

"But do not the gods want their flocks to come home? Do you think they are angry when you keep their servants from the Field of Reeds?" I was in a contemplative mood this evening.

"If the gods have gifted us with the ability to do something about our situation, we should not hesitate to use the tools they have made available to aid us in our works."

I shift uncomfortably. "I heard one of the other priests saying the only tools we should rely on are the holy spells, incantations, and prayers, rather than 'mere butchery.'" The quoted words roll strangely off my tongue.

"What may look like an act of butchery to some can in fact be a life-saving procedure to the person it is being performed on."

"But is it not the will of the gods if a person becomes injured or sick?"

Straightening, he puts his tools away into his wooden chest and turns to me. "You recall the words of our occupation?"

"'This is an ailment which I will treat,' 'this is an ailment with which I will contend,' and 'this is an ailment not to be treated,'" I recite.

"Precisely. The gods have left that judgment to us. I believe that we must do everything in our power to help *the person in front of us. Incantations and spells have their uses, as they speak not only to the gods, but to the patient's thoughts — another extremely powerful force."* He lowers his voice. *"However, sometimes they are not enough and we must find other ways to accomplish our duty. Besides"* — he winks — *"it is better to space out the arrivals, don't you think?"* I giggle. *"I, for one, do not wish to be kept waiting in line after that journey!"*

Shaking my head to clear it, I step toward Reb, who doesn't quite keep from flinching at my expression, but instead move past him, unwilling to sacrifice my place and purpose here for the satisfaction at seeing his face as I take him to the ground.

"Those are false words." I keep my chin level. "My father had nothing but the utmost respect for the gods."

"Then why did they let him and your mother burn?" he purrs softly in my ear, just as I go by.

My elbow jabs out sharp and deep in his ribs before I can stop it and a startled *whoosh* of breath erupts from his lungs. A few of the boys urge Reb to strike me as I turn sideways, not wanting to expose my back to the enemy. Paser slips between us but we have already caught the attention of sharp-eyed Ahmes.

"What is happening here?" he says, striding over, as the circle of boys magically dissipates. My heart, already racing at the confrontation, gallops faster at his approach.

"We were just debating the merits of pig dung versus donkey dung in ridding the body of unwanted parasites," Paser says smoothly.

Ahmes looks from Reb to me, taking in my clenched fists and what must be a flushed face as well as Reb's wheezing as he struggles to get his wind back. "I take it both Sesha and Reb have strong opposing opinions?" he says, tone dry. "I'll leave the three of you to finish your discussion while sweeping the temple floors."

My heart trips and tumbles down a sandbank, landing upside down in my stomach. There goes my chance of joining the hunt! I shoot Ahmes a pleading look, but he remains unmoved.

"You will find the equipment over there." He points off into the eastern corner of the temple. "I expect the floor clean enough to operate on." Turning, he motions to his scribes to pick up the baskets of transformed intestines and follow him out of the temple.

Fury at letting my emotions rob me of my chance to join the hunt clashes with fear at what could happen on the evening's excursion. I consider ignoring Ahmes completely and sneaking out after him. Instead I take a breath, giving my head a shake to clear it. Ky will be fine. The instinct to watch over him has become deeply ingrained; I need to relinquish its grip some, for both his sake and mine.

I set to work, broom in hand, pushing the bristles against the floor like I'm wiping the smirk off Reb's face. Though, he isn't smirking now — it's more of a steady glower, emanating from the other side of the room. Paser, the casualty of our brief encounter, whistles as he pushes the broom past.

"What are you so content about?" I ask, irritated. "You do not deserve to be tasked with these chores."

"Your arrival has made things around here much more interesting. That in and of itself is enough reason to be in good spirits." He grins. "Besides, I've been waiting for my chance to see the bodies up close."

My broom clatters to the floor. "What bodies?"

Paser sees my face. "Not your parents, Sesha," he hastens to say. "The ones they'll be using to demonstrate the mummification process."

My stomach rolls over. "Where are they being kept?"

"In the embalming room, of course." Paser looks at Reb. "Are you coming?"

The temple is darkening, most of the activity ceasing for the day as the priests retire for the evening.

"What is your hurry?" Reb looks uneasy. "We will see them tomorrow."

"I will accompany you," I say, heart thumping like the hind leg of a hare. With most of the scribes gone for the evening, there might be an opportunity to lose Paser and make my way to my father's study.

"Me, too." Reb straightens and shoots me a challenging look brimming with defiance.

I stifle my scoff as we finish our sweeping. Reb is a fly. Annoying, but harmless.

We put away our brooms, walk to the edge of the room, and turn down a long hallway. Torches flicker, illuminating the ceiling above painted with stars and clouds to mimic the night sky. The walls are decorated with the kings of the past, presenting their offerings to the gods. We do not talk, not wishing to attract unwanted attention.

Paser stops at the entrance to a large chamber. "This way," he says, beckoning us over, voice hushed.

"Are we allowed to be here?" I ask, eyeing the purple curtain draping down to the floor, a cloth barrier between us and the room's silent occupants.

"Why, are you frightened?" Reb asks, conveniently forgetting his earlier resistance to the expedition.

A feeling of uncertainty *has* been making itself known during our trek to the room, not of what we will find, but of what could happen if we are discovered. Or more accurately, if I am found alone in Nebifu's chambers. Not that it matters, I am going either way. But still, one likes to be prepared.

"What will happen if we are caught?" I ask Paser, ignoring Reb.

"There is no one to catch us," Paser says, neatly sidestepping my question. "The remaining priests are all involved in the sacrificial closing ceremony at the other end of the temple." He walks into the large room, Reb following behind him.

A slight noise farther down the hall attracts my ear. Whipping my head toward the sound, I strive to come up with an adequate excuse to explain our presence.

No one is there.

Must be one of Reb's rats. Taking a quick breath, I push aside the curtain and step into the room.

15

I TAKE A STEP CLOSER TO the bodies. I have seen many with their *Ba* and *Ka* departed before, but it is always an adjustment, where one expects to see life, to see only an empty shell.

"Who are they?" I ask. Despite Paser's assurance that they are not my parents, it is the bodies of a man and woman who lie there, similar in colouring and age, though the features are different enough.

"One of the nobles and his wife," Paser answers. "They will be embalmed and then placed in one of the smaller tombs with the items they will need for the afterlife."

"One of the mastabas?" I ask. This is where Queen Anat said my parents are resting. I step closer. The woman's hair is like my mother's: long, dark, and silky, falling past her shoulders. It's all too easy to imagine that it *is* my mother.

A scream claws its way up my chest into my throat like an animal trying to escape its confines. An overwhelming urge to flee washes over me and suddenly all I can think of is that I must find Ky. He is all I have left. I need to make sure he is safe *right now*. The scroll will have to wait one more day.

Whirling, I turn and start for the exit. "I have to go."

"You will be a poor physician if you cannot abide a body or two," Reb calls after me.

"Where are you going?" Paser asks.

"To hunt a hippo." Pushing past the purple curtain, I do not wait to hear their reaction.

It is almost fully dusk as I race past the marketplace, the golden disk in the sky sunk low and heavy, like a woman near her time.

"You won't find them," a voice calls behind me. I look over my shoulder to see Paser hurrying to catch me.

"I have to try," I say, knowing that he is probably right. "My brother is with them."

He reaches my side. "They will be by the water's edge, most likely on the outskirts of the town."

"Or on the water. Someone may have seen the boats leave from the docks."

"Let us go, then."

"You need not come with me," I say, looking up at him. "Ahmes will be most unimpressed."

"I know." Paser grins. "But why miss out on a chance to witness the hunt?"

"I am not sure why men need to kill a creature to prove their superiority," I say as our pace increases again.

"Not all men." Paser looks at me. "You know there is great meaning in the expedition?"

"Of course," I say dismissively. "But that doesn't mean I want my brother dying for the sake of a symbolic story." Everyone knows that hippos, often associated with chaos, are dangerous, unpredictable, and lethal beasts. When a pharaoh or prince successfully hunts the aggressive animal, he is considered to be defending his lands from this chaos and maintaining *Ma'at*, the order of the world — his most important duty as king.

Paser glances sidelong at me. "Most would be grateful for the honour to be by the young prince's side. He will one day be pharaoh, you are aware?"

"If he manages to survive long enough," I mutter.

We walk through the village. The wind has picked up and dust swirls around our ankles. With any luck there will be a storm and the hunt will be called off. But I know it will not. The dust only adds to the challenge, making things more dangerous. In return, the pharaoh and the prince will be beheld as that much braver. More powerful.

Men. I sniff.

"Do you smell something?" Paser asks.

"No, I …" I stop short and sniff the air again. There *is* a scent in the air. The smell of eggs rotting in the hot sun. "Hippo," I say, keeping my voice low, straining my ears. A large group of people is attempting to move quietly just off in the bushes, but every crack of a stick, every murmur, is as loud as a shout, announcing their location.

"Over there." I nod to Paser. The golden disk is almost fully down; the sky is a light purple, streaked with orange and pinks. We have reached the banks of the Nile.

"Watch out for crocodiles," I whisper over my shoulder.

"Crocodiles?"

A deep grunt and snort to our right cuts off my response and has the hairs on my arms standing on end. Forget the crocodiles.

"Did you hear that?" Paser whispers. There is another snort and a large *whuff* of air, meant as a warning, like the growl of a lion. But the outline of the shape looming just behind Paser is ten times larger than that of a lion.

"Don't. Move," I say, voice barely audible.

"For the glory of the gods!" A high voice ululates as men charge out of the bush, spears waved high.

I look around frantically, trying to spot Ky, praying I will not see him. Paser is frozen to the spot, eyes wide.

"Paser," I shout, urging him to follow me. "This way." The hunters stampede past us, throwing their spears at the hulking shape directly behind him. He doesn't move.

An even louder roar fills my ears and the ground quakes as the massive hippo lowers its head and paws the ground, bone-crushing jaws and deadly incisors ready to gouge anything in its path. Unfortunately, this happens to be Paser.

Ducking my shoulder low, I run at Paser with all my strength, knocking him out of the path of the charging beast. My body tenses, anticipating the sharp stab of tusks or the trampling of limbs under its heavy bulk. But the only things that graze me as the animal thunders by are a few wiry hairs. A whiff of hot rank breath envelops us both as we tumble over. The force with which I'd flung myself at Paser causes us to roll across the ground and down the banks of the river.

We land with a *splash* beside a patch of long papyrus reeds. My feet scramble to find bottom and scale back up the riverbank as fast as possible. The crocodiles I warned Paser about like nothing better than lurking among the lush grasses of the water's edge — their yellow-green eyes just above the surface, as they wait for an easy meal to present itself, much as we had.

Luckily, it isn't deep here and my feet touch, digging into the sand and rocks, each toe thrusting like one of the spears above to find purchase. A face appears over the bank and peers down, then another, giving a low whine.

"Sesha?" Ky says, voice disbelieving. Anubis lets out a happy bark.

"Ky, thank the gods you are safe! What are you doing out here?" I demand, though I know very well.

"What are *you* doing?" he asks pointedly.

"We were looking for you."

"We?" He looks puzzled.

Only then do I notice that Paser is not beside me. Only seconds have passed since we rolled over the riverbank and into the dark, wet confusion. In the light of the rising moon, I glimpse the white of his *shendyt*, the kilt that normally hangs neatly from his waist, swirling languidly in the flowing Nile.

Turning, I jump back into the water and grab him. He is unconscious. His eyelids flutter and there is a large gash bleeding at his temple. His head must have hit a rock when we rolled down the bank. He is heavy, especially with his soaked clothing dragging him down into the river.

Even though the water is not deep here, it is still awkward pulling him up onto the sandy bank. Grunting with effort, I manage to get him into a position where he's leaning back against the rocks, and kneel anxiously beside him.

He is not breathing.

16

QUICK, QUICK, QUICK.

Did Paser swallow any water? I whack his back a few times, a crude but usually effective treatment.

Nothing.

I mumble a curse that would've shocked my mother and lay him on his back, tilting his chin up slightly toward the indigo sky. Pinching his nostrils closed, I cover his mouth with mine and blow hard. Still nothing.

I blow a few more times, alternating between smacking my fist down hard on his chest. "Breathe, Paser." No response. With a frustrated cry I bring both fists down folded together, on his breastbone, with all my strength. He coughs then, sputtering out river droplets, eyes flying open. I offer a heartfelt thanks to the gods.

"What … happened?" He coughs again, as I roll him onto his side so he can spit out the rest of the water.

"Hippo." I sit back beside him, drained, as Ky scurries the rest of the way down the embankment. Shouts and unearthly howls from above have me thinking this is as good a place as any for him.

"How did you come to be here?" Ky asks, checking me over for any injuries. Anubis bounds gracefully down the slope.

I wave a half-hearted hand, reassuring him I am in one piece. Then, remembering Paser's injury, I lean over to examine him. He winces as I probe the wound gently. It is superficial, but the head bleeds a lot and my hand is covered when I pull it back. The smell of blood is sharp on the wind, whether it is all Paser's or from the hippo above, I am not sure. What I *am* sure of is this: if there is not a crocodile nearby now, there will be one very soon.

Most likely more than one.

Scrambling to my feet, I look at Ky. "Help me with him." We each put a shoulder under Paser's arms and hoist him up to his feet. "I wanted to make sure you were safe," I say to Ky, in answer to his previous question on how we came to be here. My eyes scan him: his health, so fragile this past month, seems rejuvenated by the recent food and care he's received at the palace.

"How thoughtful of you," Ky says. "But as you can see, I am fine."

Paser attempts to stand on his own and sways. Ky and I grab him before he falls. The reeds swish from side to side with an unnatural rhythm, catching my eye. Anubis lets out another low whine.

"Let's move," I say. The three of us start to make our way up the embankment, an awkward trio. "You might have been killed by that beast," I say to Ky, glancing over my shoulder. The surface of the water ripples. Maybe from a loose stone, kicked down in our climb. Maybe not.

"From what I saw, it seemed like you two were the ones in danger." Ky's tone is scolding. "Hunting hippos is dangerous work."

My mouth hangs open. "I was going to tell *you* that."

"I was with men who were armed," he pants out as we struggle up the embankment, grabbing at grasses and whatever we can to heave our bodies up the incline.

"That does not guarantee your safety." I exhale as, at last, we reach the top.

"Sesha, when is our safety ever guaranteed?" Ky says.

"He makes a point," Paser admits, flopping to the ground. The commotion of the hunt has moved off to the left. It sounds like the hippo is not making things easy for its attackers.

"You should be back at the palace," I say to Ky, after introducing them and giving Paser another once-over. Aside from the cut on his head, he appears to be all right.

"My place is beside Tutan," Ky says, stiffening with what I realize is pride and anger. "This hunt symbolizes his approaching manhood, and I am missing it."

"I did not ask you to come help," I say, crossly. Anubis comes up beside me with a low whine, head nudging into my hand, and I rub between his ears.

"Though it is much appreciated, young Ky," Paser assures him.

"And I did not ask for yours," Ky shoots back at me. "I am not a child." He spins around and walks off in the direction of the ferocious noises. Anubis gives me an apologetic look and trots after him, tongue lolling.

"Ky!" I shout, bewildered.

"Let him go." Paser puts a hand on my shoulder.

"With a deranged hippopotamus running amok?" Shrugging out from under his grasp, I follow Ky. There is a booming crash and the earth trembles. It sounds very much like a hippo toppling over onto the ground. Victorious shouts and hoots go up. Ky takes off running in the direction of the ruckus, Anubis barking at his heels.

"Ky!" I race after him.

We run up and over a small hill. Higher in the sky now, the moon basks the skirmish in a pale glow. Hunters surround the massive fallen creature. Spears stick out from its tough hide as the warriors throw nets over it, pinning it to the ground. Pharaoh stands back watching, the young prince at his side. He pulls a sharp dagger from the scabbard at his waist and presents it to Tutan, who holds it aloft, a look of excitement and fear in his eyes.

Ky and Anubis hurry down toward them. I stay, not wanting to interfere with the proceedings. At this delicate moment, a distraction could be fatal.

Tutan sees their approach, nodding at Ky, and together they approach the dying beast. The hunters stand back, in deference to their future king. They do not lower their spears, however, and I notice the ones holding down the nets grip them more tightly as Tutan walks up to the beast.

"I, Prince Tutan, do take thy life in the name of Osiris and his son, Horus." His voice trembles only slightly as he crouches, preparing to inflict the final wound.

The thick skin of a hippo does not give way easily and a considerable amount of force must be used to pierce it. I feel sympathy for the creature as it lets out another low grunt, the life force leaving her body. For it is a she; I see the teats hanging low, where multiple offspring may have nursed. Hippos might be associated with chaos but they are also renowned for being fiercely protective of their young. Briefly, I wonder if her children are fully grown or if they still need their mother. What will happen to them?

They will either survive or they won't, a cold voice says at the back of my mind. I shiver.

Tutan plunges the dagger with all his strength up into the throat of the hippo. The blade, sharpened to the point where a floating strand of hair would slice in two on contact, sinks into the animal. The beast emits one final bellow, its body shuddering, then relaxes into horrible stillness.

A great cry goes up from the crowd below. My cheeks are wet and I sense Paser's presence behind me.

"He is all right," he says softly.

"Is he?" I whirl and start back for the palace.

Back at the palace there is great jubilation and much celebration over the success of the hunt. I know I should be relieved that no one was severely injured, but I cannot shake my feeling of unease. Maybe it was the bodies at the temple earlier that affected me so?

"Sesha," a commanding voice calls on my way to the handmaidens' quarters. Turning, I see Merat walking toward me. "Are you coming to the feast?" She eyes my slightly dripping, mud-splattered clothes.

"I should go and study, Your Highness." I make a small bow, noting she is dressed for the party in fine pleated linens, a collar of gold around her neck decorated with coral and turquoise beads. Her eyelids are painted with vivid green malachite.

"I will not hear of it." She shakes her head, tiny individual braids swinging. "Besides, you need to reacquaint yourself with your table manners before the Festival of the Inundation next week. People are coming from all over the land: nobles, their families

… potential suitors." She casts me a sidelong glance.

"I have no interest in parties, Your Highness." Or suitors, for that matter. I need to focus my energies on finding the scroll.

"Come, now. You wouldn't want to offend the gods, would you?" She gives me another look, this one punctuated by an arched brow. I freeze. Reb accused my father of the very same thing this day. And the reason for the unease I'm feeling becomes clear, having been masked by the evening's events.

"It is said your father offended the gods …"

So there *has* been talk among the scribes, which means someone at the temple knows something about my parents' accident.

"No, Your Highness, of course not," I say.

"My father has declared this year's holiday to last for sixteen nights."

Probably to distract everyone from the possibility of an upcoming war. Yet even as I think this uncharitable thought, I know the festival is the highlight of most people's year. There has been much talk of it this past moon in the markets, at the docks, and around the temples. After seeing the difficulty of some of the kingdom's subjects' lives, I can easily see why this is so. With their fields submerged, farmers and their families are freed from their daily labours. This is their time to celebrate, offer tribute, and pay respect to their gods and Pharaoh. A time also to beseech the higher powers if the harvest is looking less than promising, something that — based on Wujat's statements — may be necessary this year. The temples, priests, and scribes are always very busy in preparation for and during the festival.

Abruptly, I stop walking. The festival. The perfect opportunity to search Nebifu's chambers and the rest of the temple for the elusive papyrus. With everyone occupied, any unsanctioned exploring will hopefully go unnoticed.

"… something for you."

I realize I have no idea what Merat just said. "My apologies, my lady. I did not quite catch that last part," I say, hoping she will not take offence.

Merat sighs and says, "Were you listening to me at all?"

The "no" slips out before I can stop myself from answering honestly. "But just the last few words. Or rather, the ones just before them."

Instead of becoming angry, Merat looks at me and nods. "This is what I like about you, Sesha. You are not afraid to speak the truth." She continues walking and I follow quickly behind her. If she only knew that I suspect her father, the pharaoh, of possibly having something to do with my parents' death. We reach the entrance to the quarters.

Merat turns and looks at me. "Go wash, then come to the feast. My father wishes to have a word with you."

Speak of the lion, and he shall appear. I swallow.

She startles me by pressing something into my hands. "And I was saying that I thought you might want this."

I look down at the amulet in my hands, encased in an ornate setting. It is an exquisite scarab beetle, carved from the deep blue of the lapis lazuli stone, flecked with gold, a protective talisman.

It was my father's.

"It was found in the ruins of the fire that took your parents," she says, voice uncharacteristically soft, much like the look now in her black-brown eyes. "I thought perhaps you would like to wear it tonight."

"Thank you, Your Highness." I bow low, not wishing her to see the tears threatening to spill over.

She gives another of her imperceptible nods and walks away, braids swishing, leaving me alone at the entrance to my chamber.

I let out a hollow laugh and the sound echoes, as empty as the passageway. "What good is a protective amulet if it cannot shield its wearer?"

My father's voice whispers to me from the other-world. *The power lies not only in the enchantment itself, Sesha, but in the person's belief in it.*

"Maybe that was your problem, Father," I whisper back. "Maybe you did not believe enough for some people."

17

I AM CHANGING INTO DRY CLOTHES when there is a commotion at the entrance of the room. Most of the other handmaidens are either off preparing for, or enjoying, the feast.

It is Kewat and Bebi. They are arguing.

"Ask her," I hear Bebi say.

"No," Kewat replies.

Bebi sighs. "You are as stubborn as a mule." She looks over at me and catches my eye, then, grabbing Kewat's arm, drags her over.

"Sesha, Kewat wishes to inquire about something."

"I do not," Kewat repeats stubbornly.

Bebi shakes her head. "It is better to know for sure."

"Know what?" I ask, having a fair idea of her question.

"Go on," Bebi makes an impatient noise.

Kewat seems to gather herself before the words rush out in a defiant burst. "Whether I am with child."

"You wish to know this?" I say, cautious.

"Would I be asking otherwise?" she snaps.

"There is a test one can do in the early days." I am surprised one of the other handmaidens has not told her of it yet. The matter must be private indeed if she is coming to me, not quite a stranger, but not quite someone who belongs.

"See." Bebi is smug. "I told you."

"What is it?" A look of hope flashes into Kewat's eyes.

"Why is it so imperative you know this very moment?" I ask, admitting to myself I am curious about her situation.

Kewat makes a face as if she has eaten some sour grapes from the courtyard. Bebi nods at her.

"I am promised to another." Kewat's tone matches her expression. "However ... if there is a chance I am with child, then perhaps my father will allow me to be with the father, whom I truly desire." She pleats her skirt, anxiously.

"The test involves gathering the seed of wheat and barley," I say. "Then you must collect the first water you make in the morning. If the seeds sprout after a few days, it is likely you will also bloom in time."

"See, that was not so difficult," chirps Bebi. "All you have to do is urinate on some seeds."

Kewat flushes dark red, but offers a mumbled, "Thanks be to you," before flouncing off.

"Maybe she will stop being so miserable with her questions answered," Bebi says.

"That might also be the result of her condition," I say. "Women can have unexpected changes in mood during this time."

"In actuality, she is like that most of the time," Bebi says, thoughtful. "Well, perhaps slightly less," she amends generously, then takes note of the pile of wet clothes at my feet. I was going to rinse them, then hang them to dry.

"Have you been swimming?" she asks, cocking her head.

"Yes. Well, no," I say. "There was an incident …"

"Where you and another scribe boy rolled into the river and had to be rescued by your brother?"

"We did not need …" My cheeks redden. "Wait, how do you know of this?"

Bebi casts her eyes to the gods. "Everyone knows, Sesha. Apparently, you decided to join the prince on his hippo hunt?"

I gulp. "Does Pharaoh know?"

"Most certainly. I believe he was the one relaying the story to the entire court after the hunt returned."

This is not good.

"They seemed most entertained by the tale." Bebi looks like she is trying not to laugh.

"I am glad the thought of me being almost mauled by a wild beast is so amusing," I say, sour expression matching Kewat's from earlier, and the laughter Bebi's suppressing trills out.

"Sesha." I turn to see Merat standing at the entrance.

"Coming, my Princess," I stammer, gathering my clothes and placing them on my mat, pulling the thin blanket overtop.

"I shall take care of that," Bebi whispers as I turn and walk toward the exit, where Merat waits. Forgiving her teasing, I send a grateful smile over my shoulder, then hurry down the corridor after the princess.

We walk halls bustling with the frenzy that surrounds a feast. People scurry here and there, carrying objects and food and furniture. A troupe of dancing girls fly by, scantily clothed and giggling. Anxious servants and giddy court members mingle, everyone doing their best to make the celebration for the royal family, and thus the gods, a memorable occasion.

"Did Pharaoh mention what it is he wants to discuss?" I ask.

"No," Merat says as we walk out into the gardens bursting with plants and palm trees. One of the servants places a flower garland around my neck. It lies on top of my amulet.

"Thank you for returning this to me, Your Highness," I say, fingering the smooth stone beetle. We turn up another path, passing by a large pool filled with mossy clumps of greenery, orange and yellow fish darting beneath lily pads.

"This way," she says, climbing the steps to the entrance hall of another great chamber. We walk into the large room. Four large columns reach up to a ceiling painted with elaborate murals. The pillars themselves are brightly painted with blue and green patterns. Endless tables of food stretch out before us. Figs, roasted antelope, stewed ostrich, wine, beer, and sweet loaves sprinkled with cinnamon. Despite Wujat's concern about possible food shortages, it appears Pharaoh is sparing no expense at his son's big moment.

The intoxicating smells mingle with the scents of the wax cones many of the guests wear on their heads. The woman in front of us puts a hand up to make sure hers is in place. As the cone melts, the wax will keep her tresses smooth and perfumed. Acrobats jump and twirl, flipping in the air as musicians play lively tunes. More servants surround the pharaoh and Queen Anat, fanning them with large plumes of feathers. Tutan is being clapped on the back and congratulated by Wujat and other high-ranking officials. I scan the crowd for Ky, but do not see him. Even little Tabira is perched by her mother, looking sombre but much improved, as her caretaker watches her charge with attentive eyes.

Merat leads me through the crowd toward the raised platform where the royal family sits. We weave in and out of people shouting, waving at friends, and helping themselves to food and drink. Though the party is large and crowded, it is only a fraction of the size of the Festival of the Inundation. Then, people will come by the thousands to celebrate the gods and petition them for a good harvest.

"Perhaps our conversation can wait for another time?" I say to Merat, anxious about what Pharaoh will have to say regarding my uninvited appearance at the hunt. "I do not want to bother His Highness in the midst of the festivities."

"All will be well," she says, walking up the dais, going to stand beside her parents.

"Sesha," someone says. I look to see Ahmes, an inscrutable expression on this face. "There you are."

I am about to apologize for disobeying his orders when a commanding voice calls out our names. "Sesha. Ahmes." Pharaoh has spotted us.

A look passes between Ahmes and me as we turn in unison, carefully making our way up the steps of the platform.

We bow low before the king of all the land, who addresses us both.

"You have my thanks for your assistance in my son's quest," Pharaoh says. His gaze focuses on me. "You must be making quite an impression at temple, my child, to be assisting Ahmes after only a few days." I look at Ahmes, unsure of what to say, but he stares straight ahead, answering for me.

"Yes." Ahmes clears his throat. "She has been proving herself a most adept student."

"I see you have your father's skill, Sesha. I cannot wait to see what secrets you will reveal to us," Pharaoh says with a significant look. I gulp. He cannot be expecting results so soon in my search, can he?

"Yes, Your Highness," I say. "I am learning much." I almost add "while dealing with distractions like hippo-hunting brothers," but something tells me he will not want excuses.

Queen Anat says something and Pharaoh leans over to confer with her, waving his hand, dismissing us.

Ahmes and I bow and walk down the steps of the platform.

"Thank you for … your help," I whisper, not quite sure why he covered for my disobedience.

Ahmes's voice is insistent. "Sesha, you must —" he begins. But just then Pharaoh stands and opens his arms to the audience, summoning Tutan to come stand by his side. The young prince is still in his hunting clothes, streaks of red smeared down his smooth thin chest and across his forehead. Ky would be impressed by the ceremony.

Ky. Where is he?

"Sesha, listen to me …" Ahmes urges again. We move off to the side of the room, past the throngs milling closer to the platform to hear Pharaoh's words.

"What is it?" I look at him. "Ky?"

"Yes," he responds tersely. "You must come at once."

18

"I KNEW HE SHOULD NOT have gone on that hunt." We hurry down one of the darkened hallways, the torches spaced out far here.

"There is no telling if it was the hunt that aggravated his condition," Ahmes says. "From what I gather, the two of you were living quite roughly until only a few days ago."

He is right. But I am still angry with myself and he senses it.

"Besides, I forbade you to accompany him. If you want someone to be irate with, then look no further," Ahmes says. He rounds a corner and after a few more moments we arrive at the infirmary, in a wing off the back of the palace.

"Ky?" I whisper, not wishing to disturb any of the other patients.

"This way." Ahmes gestures to the end of a row, empty except for one small form. I assume no one else is sick enough to miss the grand celebration. This only increases my worry. Ky would not miss Tutan's moment unless something was seriously wrong.

"Sesha?" Ky looks up from his mat, bleary-eyed.

"What happened?" I kneel beside him.

"I do not know," Ky admits. "The last thing I remember is Tutan slaying the hippo. Then both of us were up in the air, being carried on the shoulders of the other hunters toward the palace."

"Ky suffered an episode where he lost consciousness and his limbs spasmed. Fortunately, one of the hunters was wise enough to lay him on the ground, away from any danger, until the convulsions passed. He is uninjured but was confused and disoriented, so I brought him here."

My hands go to his head. I feel his skull pulsating under my fingers.

"It is getting worse?" I ask, more of a statement than a question. I've witnessed the uncontrollable jerking of his extremities during these episodes. It's scary, but he's generally all right after they pass. I wonder what the soldier thought? Most likely that a demon had possessed him.

"My head feels as if it will burst," Ky says, voice small.

"The pressure must be increasing," Ahmes says.

"We must relieve it." I look at Ahmes. "What can we do?"

"Not much without surgery," Ahmes admits. "The scroll is our best hope. Your father mentioned there were several cases on it that refer to the head and its contents. It may describe a treatment or incantation that has been lost to us since Imhotep's time."

Ky attempts to sit up. "The pain is already subsiding. I must join Tutan."

"You are not going anywhere," I say.

Ky's eyes flash. "I am."

I let out a frustrated sigh. "You need to rest."

"All lying here does is make me think about how awful I feel," he retorts. "At least at the party with Tutan I will be distracted from my discomfort."

"Can you even walk?" I demand.

He gets up to demonstrate, swaying, much as Paser did earlier on the riverbank. Then, righting himself, he staggers up and down the row of mats, wincing only slightly.

"See?" he turns and puts his hands on his hips.

"You are as stubborn as a goat," I say, exasperated. "Fine, but you must tell me the moment you start feeling unwell again."

He looks up at me, expression bleak. "There is nothing you can do, Sesha. This is an ailment you cannot treat."

"I will treat it," I say firmly. "And I swear by the gods I will find that scroll and see you cured."

The next morning, I check on Ky, who seems to be much improved. Ahmes had given me some juniper and marjoram oils, which I administer with a gentle scalp massage to reduce any lingering pain and in the hopes of encouraging some fluid to drain. As I walk into temple the smell of the juniper on my fingers merges with the burning incense.

Walking past the giant obelisks, I think upon my brother's condition, which only started this past year. He contracted a dreadful illness, suffering from fever, a stiff neck, and terrible head pain. With Father's constant care he survived the sickness, but it left fluid inside his skull, causing swelling, which has been steadily worsening. I know Father feared it might eventually kill Ky; that's why he was so consumed with the scroll.

If the document was indeed written by Imhotep, the greatest physician of all time, it might hold crucial information that will ensure a successful outcome. As Ahmes pointed out, it could describe an innovative procedure or special technique that has been lost or forgotten over the years, one that can save Ky's life. I cannot wait for the festival. I must get into Nebifu's chambers at once.

I hurry past several priests into the inner chamber where some of the junior scribes have surrounded a gesticulating Paser. There is a dressing on his temple, covering his wound from the night before. They are inquiring how he came by his injury.

I go to my spot and reach for my instruments.

They are not there.

Panic flutters in my chest. I lift my mat, thinking back to the night before. I am sure I placed them there, just before going with Paser and Reb to see the …

Reb.

Straightening, I look for him but he is nowhere to be found. I march over to Paser and the group.

"Where is Reb?"

"He is not here today?" Paser looks around.

"It appears not." My hands are on my hips. "And neither are my writing tools."

A loud clap has the group dissipating and everyone taking their seats, me reluctantly.

"Today we will be learning more about the complex process of mummification," Sebau says brusquely. "Have your writing instruments ready, as you will be taking detailed notes of this process. Everyone follow me."

Everyone grabs their things and starts down the hallway toward the room with the bodies I saw last night. Giving a last desperate look around for my tools, I follow the group, empty-handed.

"One must show utmost respect for the dead at all times," Sebau says over his shoulder as we trail down the hall. "You are the only group of students permitted to observe this sanctified process."

This is one of the changes my father implemented. For much of the past, medical scribes had naught to do with those who did the embalming. But Father felt much could be learned by examining a body. With him gone, who knows how long they will keep up this practice? Sebau stops in front of the entrance to the room and gives us a stare as hard and cold as the walls of a tomb. "As you are training in the medical arts, *some* think the best way to learn about the body is to observe it closely. That being said, any inappropriate behaviour and expect the stick." He pulls back the curtain and enters the room.

Preparing myself, I step past the curtain, hoping the bodies will not affect me as they did last night. Both have been stripped and washed with sweet-smelling wine and water from the Nile. While it is not as difficult viewing the corpses in the light of day, I cast my eyes around for something else to look upon.

Farther back in the room there is a large pile of items. Glinting gold, silver, and shimmering stones adorn a giant pile of treasures, stacked carefully on top of each other. These are the items the couple will need for the afterlife, to sustain them and their spirits. In addition to the usual assortment of gems and charms, there are other beautiful objects such as bejewelled musical instruments — including one splendid reed — stunning statues, intricate pottery, and furniture, almost reaching the ceiling. Though I am used to seeing much wealth in the palace, it is quite something to see so many valuable objects heaped together in a mountain of glittering riches.

It is no wonder the priests have a difficult time keeping thieves away. There have been a few infamous robberies in recent years, of some of the more prominent nobles' tombs, including a few of the ancient pharaohs and their families. Thieves made off with many irreplaceable and precious items. I remember Father grumbling under his breath at the latest one, a great king from the past. He wondered how the robbers were able to get by the guards, and how they knew exactly where to look, deliberating with Mother whether they might have had inside help. The criminals still have not been caught. And a good thing for them — robbing the graves of the dead is a most heinous crime, resulting in execution by impalement, or worse, being burned alive. This ensures the wrongdoers will have no body to pass into the afterlife with. I shudder, tormented at the thought of my parents sharing the same fate. Perhaps they will not be there when Ky and I arrive in the Field of Reeds.

In the midst of my distress, Reb materializes in the group, catching my shudder.

"Scared, Sesha?" he says with a quiet sneer.

"It is you who should be scared," I whisper back, fierce as a lioness. "What have you done with my tools?"

A smirk of satisfaction crosses his face and he opens his mouth to reply.

"Shut your mouths!" Sebau barks at us. "Did I not say the utmost respect must be paid during this process?" His eyes narrow on Reb. "And why are *you* late this morning, might I ask?"

"The clouds … they … they … blocked the sun's rays, so I was not woken in time." Reb looks down at the floor. There are new bruises high on his left arm, next to a vicious-looking scar.

Sebau looks as if he is about to reprimand him further, but just then two priests walk into the room. One carries a long metal rod with a hooked end, and the other holds a sharp blade. They walk over to the bodies lying on the concrete slabs. Sebau monotonously takes us through the process. Bulging wicker baskets rest under the tables, filled with a salt called natron, which will cover the bodies for forty days, sucking out all moisture. They will then be stuffed with pleasant-smelling spices and linen to give them back their shape, covered with oils and resins, and adorned with protective amulets and any other jewels or items the nobles requested to be buried with. Then the bodies will be carefully wrapped in strips of linen and each one will be placed into intricately painted human-shaped coffins.

The priests each stand at a body, ready to begin the work of preparing and preserving it for the afterlife. The first priest holds his rod aloft and begins muttering an incantation. Most of the protective spells will be said in the final stages, when the linen bandages are applied, but perhaps the prayer is for him, to ready him for the grisly task ahead.

We watch in silence, breath held, as the priest takes the rod and shoves it, hard, up the nobleman's left nostril. There is a sickening crunch as he breaks through the nasal cavity and the hooked end of the rod sinks deep into the skull. He moves the instrument in a forceful, circular motion, pulverizing the tissues in the head. Sweat breaks out on his brow after a few moments of jamming the rod in and out, swirling the contents around. Once the priest perceives them mushy enough, he begins to withdraw them through the nostrils, using the hooked end of the rod.

Piece by piece, chunk after chunk of spongy pink and grey matter is extracted through the nose. Each time the priest inserts the rod, he pulls out more and more of the squishy material, scooping it onto the tray beside the body. While he finishes his task, the other priest steps up to the body of the woman.

He makes a swift and deep incision into her left side. This is where he will extract the vital organs from. I momentarily avert my gaze from the grim proceedings. Eight elaborate containers rest on a table behind the priests, each one finely carved from limestone. These special jars are meant for the liver, the intestines, the lungs, and the stomach. The heart will be left inside the body. In the afterlife, it will be weighed against a feather so the person's life can be judged by Osiris. A wicked person's heart is heavy and is immediately gobbled up by Ammit, the Devourer. If the person has lived a good and honest life, as proven by their light heart, they will be allowed to enter the Field of Reeds, the beautiful and sunny kingdom of Osiris. There, people are surrounded by golden wheat and fruit trees, able to eat, drink, and be happy for all of eternity. If they make it there, that is.

My attention is drawn back to the pile of pink and grey juicy tissue. The brains, having no important function, will be disposed of. Father strongly disagreed with this practice, feeling that there is much about the organ that we do not fully understand. He had witnessed injuries to the head, which resulted in a person losing the ability to walk or talk. And then there is Ky's condition, as well.

There is a loud *thump* and we look over. One of the other students has fainted. Sebau lets out a loud sigh.

"One in every class," he mutters, clapping his hands. "That is enough for today. You will go back to the main room and record your observations. Paser, Reb, pick him up and take him outside for some air."

Obediently we line up to file out, leaving the priests to their messy tasks. Paser and Reb walk over to the fallen student, who has swooned next to a pile of cloth rags. Too bad he didn't sway a little more to the right; it would have been a softer landing.

Reb kicks the pile of rags aside with his foot. Suddenly, Paser lets out a shout. Heads turn and I catch the angry hiss of what sounds like a very large snake.

19

MORE SHOUTS ERUPT AS PANIC spreads through the room, quicker than a fire through dry fields. Everyone runs for the exit. Everyone but Paser, Reb, and the fallen boy, who are trapped by the muscular body of the scaly brown snake, which rears up indignantly out of the heap of rags. Though normally shy, cobras are fiercely hostile when cornered. This one is not happy about being disturbed and rises to full height, flaring its hood and flicking its tongue with another sinister hiss.

Paser and Reb are frozen.

And with good reason. A single bite from a cobra has enough venom to kill an elephant. I used to milk Apep regularly, lessening but not completely removing the danger in working with her. She also knew that striking my hard reed would only cause her pain, so would hesitate to do so. This specimen will not have had the same training.

The boy comes to in all the commotion. Sitting up with a dazed look on his face, he looks around for clues as to what is happening. As he catches sight of the hissing, looming snake, his eyes roll back in his head and he promptly passes out again.

Without thinking, I run to the pile of the nobles' riches, snatching the bejewelled reed I noticed earlier. Carved from bamboo, the instrument is dotted with semi-precious stones. Putting it to my lips, I begin to play, quickly moving the flute-like instrument in arcs to capture the snake's attention. A cobra's reach is about one third of its body length, and I make sure to stay well out of range, moving hypnotically from side to side. It begins to sway along with me. Out of the corner of my eye, I see Paser and Reb each grab a leg of the unconscious boy and slowly inch themselves out of harm's way.

Cobras are often reluctant to strike; they subscribe to the thought that the best offence is a showy defence. Slowly, still playing the instrument, I walk backward in the direction of the tables. The cobra eyes me warily as I retreat. Putting the instrument down, I grab one of the baskets and tip it on its side. Salt spills out silently onto the floor, spreading underneath the embalming tables. Grabbing a handle of the empty basket, I walk it back toward the cobra, moving as cautiously as possible. Leaving the basket there on its side, I back away again. The cobra will want a safe, cool, and dark environment to escape to after all the chaos. Withdrawing from the room, I reach the exit, bumping into Paser, who whispers excitedly in my ear.

"Sesha, that was incredible!"

"Well done, child," Sebau says, his voice slightly shaky.

I shrug. "The snake would rather eat a toad than me. He only felt threatened. Soon he will crawl into the basket and fall asleep and then we can remove him."

"Class is adjourned for the rest of the day, while we deal with our … visitor," Sebau says. More priests have come down the hallway to see what all the noise is about.

The boy who lost consciousness has once more been revived. "What happened?" he mumbles.

"It appears there is a charmer in our midst, Djaty," Reb says to the fainter, but his usual look of disdain has been replaced by one of wariness. Without another word, he turns and walks down the hallway.

"I am starving," Paser says, clapping me on the back. "Nothing like unexpected danger to wake the appetite. Let us go find something to eat."

The group disperses and I follow him to the room where food is kept on hand for the priests and temple scribes. We fill our plates as others file in behind us. Some of the boys are teasing the rattled Djaty, while others congratulate me as the story of my exploit grows more harrowing by the second. Embarrassed by the attention, I turn to Paser.

"I would like to get some air."

"I will accompany you and you can tell me where you learned to handle a snake like that," Paser says.

We turn and walk out through the halls, holding our dishes. Reb appears as we approach the outer room of the temple. He, too, is holding something in his hands.

"My tools," I say, heart leaping.

"I should not have taken them," Reb says abruptly, handing them to me. With a quick bow of his head he walks off, heading in the direction of the food. And that is probably as close to an apology as I will get from him.

"I am surprised he returned them," I say.

"He is probably scared of you." Paser grins. "What you did back there probably has a lot of people wondering if you have been blessed by the gods."

I think again, as I so often do, of my parents. "If so, they have a most peculiar way of showing it," I say, trying to keep the edge out of my voice.

We walk out into the sunshine and head to the garden off the side of the temple where many of the fruits and vegetables are grown. Finding a place to sit on a stone bench, we eat in companionable silence.

I am the one to break it. "The gods have little to do with it. It was my father who taught me how to" — I struggle to find the correct word — "to bond with the snake. Despite their divine connections, they are just creatures like you and me, and as we want to be treated with respect, so do they."

Paser must catch the forlorn echo in my voice. "Your father was a most impressive man. Have you been to visit his tomb yet?"

"No," I say, looking at my half-eaten food. "Queen Anat mentioned they are in one of the mastabas, but I am not sure which one." The necropolis is vast and complex and lies on the west bank of the Nile where the sun goes down and enters the underworld. My eyes are drawn in that direction, looking past the other students milling about. The action with the snake has everyone taking a break and there's a distractedness in the air that comes after an unexpected commotion. A distractedness that could be taken advantage of …

"I know where they are," Paser says.

I look up at him, heart soaring then plummeting all in one breath. As much as I want to visit my parents I cannot let another opportunity to look for the scroll slip through my fingers.

"Do you want me to show you?" he asks.

"That would be most kind of you," I say. The rush of subduing the cobra lingers in my veins, emboldening me. "But first there is something I must ask Nebifu."

If Paser thinks anything odd of my errand he does not let it show. "I will wait here," he says. Placing my plate on the bench beside me, I leave before I can change my mind.

20

SCRIBES STROLL THE HALLWAYS, and though it is not unreasonable for me to walk the temple at this time of day, I keep my eyes down. Slowing my pace, I reach the corridor leading to one of the inner chambers, glancing around to make sure no one is watching. In a blink of an Eye of Ra, I turn down the corridor. The gods of luck must be with me because it is empty. My feet are light as I approach the thick door of my father's old study. With a quick intake of breath to steady myself, I rap sharply on the wood.

No answer.

I rap again, a little louder. There is no "come in" or any sound at all to indicate its inhabitant is present. Cautiously, I push on the door and it creaks open a crack. Poking my head in, I call out softly.

"Your Holiness?" Nothing. Pushing the door all the way open, I look up to make sure I am still unobserved, then slink into the room.

Like Ahmes's chambers, it is mostly unchanged from when my father occupied it, though some time has passed since then. Running my fingers along the shelves, I look closely for anything that might resemble the scroll. Minutes pass while I scour the room, but nothing sticks out as a likely candidate. Would Nebifu's chambers have been searched, as well? No wonder the priest seems to resent Wujat, the implication being that he is not bright — or honest — enough to recognize or reveal the scroll of his own accord.

It is not here. Frustration rips through me and I slam both hands down on the desk with such force that the blow echoes through the sanctified chamber. Just then, voices reach me from the corridor, increasing in volume as they get closer. Wildly casting my eyes around for somewhere to hide, I settle on a large wardrobe at the back of the room. Its door closes behind me just as Reb and his uncle walk into the study.

"What were you thinking, being late this morning?" Nebifu berates his nephew.

"I am sorry, Uncle," Reb mumbles as I peer through the slim crack in the wardrobe.

"Do you have any idea how it looks when my own … relation … cannot even make it to his classes on time?" His Holiness is incensed.

"It will not happen again, Uncle." Reb looks past his uncle, eyes flickering over the wardrobe. I stop breathing.

"Leave my sight." Nebifu waves his hand in disgust. "I will deal with you when we get home." Reb doesn't wait around to be asked again.

"Stupid boy," Nebifu mutters. "As if I do not have enough on my dish with Pharaoh and Wujat searching for that blasted scroll …" My heart leaps like a gazelle as he rummages around in his desk for something. Is he about to reveal the missing document? But instead of a papyrus, he pulls out a small jug and takes a few healthy swallows, then leaves the room. Letting out a sigh I climb out of the stifling wardrobe and spend a few more precious seconds looking for the scroll, to no avail. It does not appear to be here after all. But even in my disappointment, I sense its nearness. It is somewhere in the temple, calling to me.

Making sure there is no one in the corridor, I exit the chambers, stealthily making my way back outside to fresh air and to Paser.

"My apologies," I say, breathless, when I reach him. "That took a little longer than expected." Paser is practising his scripts on some ostraca.

"Did you manage to speak with Nebifu?" he asks, curious.

"He was not … available." I smooth down my robe, brushing away dust and the cloistering smell of Nebifu's wardrobe.

Paser puts away his tools. "Do you still wish to visit your parents?"

Not trusting myself to speak, I give a slight nod.

Perhaps they will be able to provide some guidance in my search. I am not having much success, and Ky is running out of time.

Paser stands and offers his outstretched hand to me. "Then let us go."

I take it and we set out for the City of the Dead.

The necropolis stretches out before us. Dozens of mastabas, flat-roofed, rectangular structures, dot the landscape. Predecessors to the Great Pyramids that lie futher along the Nile, they are hallowed tombs for the dead, though not nearly as impressive in size as those guarded by the equally imposing Sphinx. My father took me to see them once; I will never forget the awe I felt looking upon the incredible structures. We leave our raft at the water's edge and weave through the paths. Many of the ancient tombs are crumbling, completely filled in with rubble, dating back from ancient dynasties. At last we reach the newer buildings.

"That one over there." Paser points off to the left but it has already caught my eye. I have been here a few times before, when I was very young, to visit the spirits of my grandparents. Mother took me. I remember asking why Father did not come. She said that he had not gotten along well with his parents, who died before I was born, but she thought it important that we pay our respects.

As we walk up to the large mastaba building, Paser speaks. "There are many rooms and chambers hidden beneath. It can be confusing. Go slow and take note of when you turn."

Paser nods at the guard at the front and we enter the main room. It is a small chapel with pictures and statues of the deceased lining the walls. Here people leave offerings and say prayers for their departed friends and family members. There are a few small lanterns lit around the room.

Paser gestures. "In here." We walk into another room. This one is brightly illustrated with the traditional scene of a person's heart being weighed against Osiris's Feather of Truth. Anubis, Ky's dog's namesake and God of the Dead, holds the man's hand, while Ammit, Devourer of the Dead, waits to see if he will be fed this day. But, alas for Ammit, the scale is balanced, guaranteeing entrance to the afterworld. Thoth, the god of wisdom and patron of scribes, records the verdict. Spells and incantations are painted on the walls, aiding the person in their journey.

"I believe your parents were the last ones to be buried here. Soon the shaft leading to where their coffins lie will be filled with stone, so that none may pass."

"And so that the tombs will not be robbed," I say. "It does not matter. I can't imagine they had much left to be buried with."

"On the contrary, it was a most spectacular procession," Paser says. "The mourning women hired to wail at the ceremony put on a most impressive performance."

"You watched?"

"You did not?"

"I could not bear it."

"Sesha." Paser puts a hand on my shoulder. "You know that for people as good as your parents, death is only the beginning of a great adventure."

"But if their bodies were not preserved," I say, at last voicing my anguish, "how will their spirits survive? How am I to see them again?"

Paser is silent for a moment. "That is maybe a question for one of the High Priests. As long as their names are inscribed on their coffins, their *Ba* and *Ka* should be able to find their way back. And it is said the spirit of a person can animate a statue. Perhaps Ra will accept these in their place and reward them with a new body in the afterlife. After all, the gods can do anything."

Paser's reasoning makes me feel slightly better. "Were statues placed in their coffins?"

"I do not know. I am sure the pharaoh would have arranged something —"

"Where are the stairs leading to the burial chambers?" I interrupt, scanning the room. "I need to see for myself." I notice the false door, where the spirits may leave and enter from, as I exit the room. After walking for a few minutes I come to a small room in the centre of the building. Steps lead steeply down into the subterranean chambers.

"They must only be entered for performing special ceremonies," Paser says, coming up behind me.

"You do not have to accompany me."

He rolls his eyes. "Has anyone told you that you are very stubborn?"

"Two people used to tell me that all the time." I grab one of the lit torches and, walking over to the stairs, place my foot on the first step leading down underground. "And they are down there." I look back over my shoulder at Paser. "Coming?"

21

THE TORCH FLICKERS AS we descend the shaft; like us, fire needs air to breathe. With hands tracing the painted walls, we go lower and lower at a gradual incline until we come to a large antechamber. Several paths lead off from the central room, each hallway bordered by two large pillars. Lifting my torch higher illuminates the words inscribed above each passageway. My family name is written above the one directly to my right.

"This way," I say to Paser. We move down the stone hall until we reach a room on the left and stop. "Here." We enter the room. The two coffins lie side by side. Despite my fear that my parents would have no possessions to be buried with, a small number of items lie around the room. A few of my father's surgical instruments, most notably his prized obsidian blade, the volcanic glass having survived the flames. Some pottery of my mother's, charred but still whole. I touch one of the bowls, and my fingers come away black with soot.

The royal family must have had them put here. I am gratified at their thoughtfulness. Perhaps I have been wrong in my suspicions.

"Help me lift the lid," I say to Paser, throat dry.

He looks at me, raising an eyebrow. "What do you expect to find?"

"I am not sure." Indeed, I do not actually know the condition of my parents' bodies. Maybe there are only ashes left. Maybe semi-charred remains. Gulping, I reconsider this course of action.

Paser echoes my thoughts. "Sesha, I think it best to let them lie in peace."

My hand rests on the heavy lid. It will take more than the two of us to put it back on.

"Maybe you are right."

"Why do you not ask Wujat if you really need to know? Was he not your father's friend?"

"Yes, he was." He is also the Grand Vizier and High Priest of all the land.

"I am sure he will tell you the details if they are so important to you."

Wujat will also want a report of how my search for the scroll is going. Glancing around, it strikes me that more than I thought was saved from the fire. Could I be mistaken about the scroll being in the temple? Maybe Father *did* keep the priceless document at home and it was overlooked in the ruins. Of course, if it was there, it is more likely it burned up in the flames, but I squash that thought.

"I need to go to my home," I say to Paser. "Or what is left of it."

It still smells like smoke. Most of the rubble has been cleared, but pops of colour peek through disintegrated bricks of mud and clay. A carved toy bird of Ky's. A broken cosmetic brush of my mother's. Sifting through the ashy wreckage, I scan the ground for clues.

"What are you looking for?" Paser asks.

"I am not sure," I admit, kicking over a broken chamber pot. "But I hope I will know when I find it."

Paser clears his throat. "I wanted to thank you. For saving my life the other night."

I look up from my scouring, offering Paser a rueful smile. "As it was I who put you in danger in the first place, you need not mention it." The wind rises, whipping up a tattered white feather that was once part of my mother's earring. It circles lazily in the air, then is caught by a stronger gust, flying off before my hand can reach out to catch it.

"Sesha, your face is white. Are you all right?"

"This has just been an … eventful day."

"Have you even had a chance to properly grieve for your parents?"

"I have mourned for them every day since their deaths." But Paser has struck upon something. Though tears have come a few times this past moon, I have never let them spill freely over. Their deaths were such a shock and then it was straight into survival mode, taking care of Ky, trying to see him safe and well and us both fed and …

Moisture gathers in my eyes. Despite my prickliness, Paser has been a good friend these past few days. He takes another step closer, resting a warm hand on my back. "It is all right to cry."

"I am afraid if I start I will not be able to stop."

He smiles, a crooked grin. "It is the season of the Inundation, the more water on the ground, the better."

I let out a choked sound that is half-laugh, half-sob. Paser wraps his arms around me and gathers me close in a hug. The tears begin in earnest then, streaming down my face; my body shakes with grief as I surrender to the pain of losing my parents, the fear of not finding the scroll in time to save Ky. Oddly, succumbing to the doubt and sadness makes me feel lighter and after a few moments the weeping subsides. I wipe my face, feeling cleansed somehow.

"Thank you," I sniffle, sitting down on a blackened brick.

"You are most welcome," he says, squatting beside me. "Keeping your emotions bottled up inside is not healthy for the spirit."

"My mother used to say that." My big toe traces an arc in the thick ashy sand. A flash of copper underfoot catches my eye. Bending down, I pick up a small circular object, covered with dust, and blow on it.

It is a ring, inscribed with the Eye of Ra. A ring worn by Pharaoh's personal guards.

"What did you find?" Paser asks.

My hand involuntarily curls around the trinket. "A ring." My mouth is dry.

Paser nods at my enclosed fist. "Was it your mother's?"

"No." Making up my mind, I inhale deeply, slowly opening my hand to reveal the incriminating band. "I think it belongs to one of the pharaoh's guards."

"What would that be doing here?" He frowns and takes it from me to examine it. My expression must reveal what I am thinking, because as he looks back at me, he gives a sharp intake of breath.

"Sesha. We may be in some trouble."

22

AFTER I FINISH TELLING PASER everything, he shakes his head.

"And you have no idea where the scroll is?" he asks, as we approach the palace.

"None." I tuck the ring safely away.

"Is it possible it was in the fire?" he asks.

"I did wonder that, but now I don't think so," I say, shaking my head. "Father would often stay late at the temple; he must have been working on it there. I just have no idea where."

"It is a big building with many places to hide." And with only one room down and many to go, I could use a little reinforcement.

"I plan to search the more accessible areas before and after classes." Looking at him under lowered lashes to gauge his reaction, I continue. "The festival should be a good time to explore … harder to reach places." Father's old study was a piece of honeycake to get into compared to some of the inner and underground chambers. "The priests will be busy and distracted, along with everyone else." Despite Nebifu's mutterings in his chamber, it remains unclear if he is involved or not; it is best to tread carefully.

Paser nods. "Yes, that is probably our best chance. In the meantime, I will keep my ears open and maybe ask some of the other scribes. Someone might have seen or heard something. And not much escapes Nebifu, though I am sure Wujat and Pharaoh have already spoken with him."

"You are going to help me, then?" Relief floods my body.

"Of course." Paser looks at me in surprise. "Why would I not?"

"It might be dangerous. If Pharaoh did have something to do with my parents' death …"

"I just cannot fathom why," Paser muses. "But I am not afraid. I believe he is a good man."

"I once thought so, too," I say as we reach the entrance to the wing where the handmaidens' quarters are. "Now I am not sure of anything anymore."

"Well, you can be sure of my friendship." Paser smiles at me and warmth filters into the cracks of my heart.

"Thank you," I say.

"Besides" — Paser smiles as he walks me to the wooden doors — "all these years studying have been very dull. Did I not say how I love a good adventure?

And how since you showed up things are a lot more exciting?"

"I am glad to be of service," I say, a matching grin spreading across my face.

"Sesha?"

I turn in surprise to see Merat standing there. "Yes, Princess?"

"I have been waiting for you," she says. But she is looking at Paser.

"My Princess." He bows.

"It is good to see you, Paser," Merat says. "I hope the gods have been keeping you well."

"I wish the same for you, Your Highness."

"No need to be so formal," she says, brushing back a piece of hair. "We were friends once."

"We are friends always," Paser says and a light flush spreads from Merat's neck up onto her smooth high cheeks.

I clear my throat. "What is it my lady wishes of me?"

"I thought we might have another lesson," she says, looking at Paser, chin high. "Sesha is teaching me to read hieratic script."

"I am sure the princess will have no trouble picking it up." Paser bows again.

"She is a quick study." I try to hide my smile. "See you tomorrow, Paser."

"Good night, Sesha." He nods formally at Merat. "Princess." Then takes his leave, striding away.

I look at Merat, who for once seems less in command of herself than usual.

"Are you all right?" I ask.

"I am to be married." She sags against the wall.

"Your parents have found a suitor so soon?" I am astonished. The last one was rejected only a few suns ago.

"To one of the Hyksos chieftains in the North," she says, tone as bitter as horehound. "Father's latest attempt to smooth things over between the warring tribes. He thinks it may turn their attention away from us."

My brain works furiously. If Pharaoh is still anticipating war, he cannot have much faith in his daughter's upcoming marriage. Unless this recent development is his last-minute attempt to buy extra time to find the scroll in preparation for battle and its consequences. The document must be even more important to him than I'd thought if he is sacrificing his own daughter.

"The princess seemed most pleased to see Paser," I say, changing the subject to distract Merat from her distress. She gives me a look as sharp as the aloe vera plant and I clap a hand to my mouth. "My apologies, Your Highness. I do not mean to seem overly familiar … I … I only wanted to see a smile, and … and it seems thoughts of him bring it," I finish lamely.

Her mouth turns up a fraction. "Am I really that obvious, Sesha?"

"No, Princess. I have just become very good at reading faces," I say, voice sincere.

"Hmmm, come then," she says, gesturing at me to follow. "Let us have our lesson and then you can tell me all about your day. I imagine it was much more interesting than mine, engagement notwithstanding."

I finish telling Merat about the snake and she laughs and shakes her head. Though I feel we are becoming something resembling confidants, I still do not mention my suspicions of her father, or the ring I found in the ashes of my home. Its shape presses against my hip bone.

"It seems you and Paser have become quite close," she says, trying, but not succeeding, to keep the dusky blush from creeping into her cheeks again. It completely changes her demeanour, making her seem more approachable.

"He has been most kind." I speak frankly, understanding what she is getting at. "But I do not need to be distracted from my studies just now." Or from my quest to find the scroll. "Paser is a good friend, nothing more."

She sighs. "My engagement is to be announced at the Festival of the Inundation."

I murmur soothing consolations to her. Poor Merat. And though it is a minor consideration on top of everything else, perhaps if I find the scroll she will not have to marry someone she does not love. Though I know love has little to do with most royal marriages, Merat, surprisingly, seems to possess the heart of a romantic under her cool exterior and I would not wish her to be unhappy.

The sun is getting low. Merat notices me shifting in my seat. "Do you need to use the chamber pot, Sesha?"

"I have not supped yet, Your Highness," I admit. My stomach lets out a loud growl and she looks amused.

"So I hear." She waves her hand. "We shall continue tomorrow. After that I am afraid there will be little time. There is much preparation to be done for the festival."

I bow and exit her chambers. There is much work for me to do, as well. But first, I must go check on my brother.

The next morning Sebau announces that we will be seeing patients with mild maladies, and a buzz of excitement runs through our group. Trailing behind the other scribes chattering about the thrill of helping real patients, I think of Ky as we walk to the village. He was in a cheerful mood last evening, playing and laughing with Tutan. I did not want to spoil his happiness by mentioning the soldier's ring, an object which may implicate his best friend's father, and so I said nothing, letting him enjoy the blissfulness that accompanies ignorance.

I am not sure what it is — maybe a sound, maybe a movement — but something rouses me from my thoughts, the hairs along my body rising in unison, as if caught in one of Set's angry desert storms. The god of chaos and violence feels close. Again, I get an inkling of being watched, sensing not only the god's eyes on me but human ones, as well. Glancing around, I notice nothing out of the ordinary and scold myself for being overdramatic, shaking off the unsettling feeling. Paser, who is talking with Reb alongside me, catches my gaze and raises his brows in a questioning look. I give my head a slight shake to show it is nothing and we continue on our way to the village.

As we reach the centre of town a small crowd is already forming around the physicians' tent. Each of us is given a satchel full of bandages and ointments, sutures and needles, tweezers, scalpels, probes, and tooth pullers.

"Welcome," Ahmes greets us. "These are your medical bags, which you are to take utmost care of. You may treat the minor wounds and injuries. Anything that looks serious, or that you are unsure of, send on to one of the senior doctors. Go and find a place to set up."

Square mud bricks are piled waist-high, each with a cloth spread over the top. We walk quickly toward the makeshift tables. I spot one in the shade and increase my pace. The sun will not shine in my eyes as strongly there, and my patients will have some relief from the heat. I get to it first and put my satchel down on the flat surface. Eagerly, I reach my hand into the bag to take out my instruments and medicines.

My fingers sink into warm spongy tissue. It is wet and soft, yet firm at the same time. An involuntary shudder runs through my body, for I know what I am touching.

Brains.

23

MY HAND SNATCHES ITSELF back as if it has met open flame. I look around to see if anyone is watching and notice Ahmes walking over.

"What is wrong?" he says.

I keep my face preternaturally calm. "Someone put something in my bag."

He upends the satchel, and though I already know what is in there, it still churns my stomach to see the pink chunks of organ fall to the ground along with the medical supplies.

Ahmes's mouth falls open. "Who did this?" he demands.

My eyes go to Reb but he is busy bandaging a wound and takes no notice of the scene. Besides, he returned my tools after the snake escapade, and, while not overly friendly this morning, he did give me a respectful nod. Perhaps one of the other students? Or someone with a more malevolent intent? Was this a harmless prank or a threat? I recall the feeling of being watched and feel a chill in spite of the humid day.

Just then a man cradling his arm walks up to Ahmes and me. He is pallid and sweating, emitting small gasps of pain.

"We will investigate this further later," Ahmes says quietly, pushing the disgusting pile aside with his foot. "Right now your duty is to the patient in front of you."

I gather myself, along with my instruments and the fallen supplies, flinging off any remaining matter, then turn to the man. His arm is badly broken. Casting my eyes around for a splint, I spot a pile of sticks lying under the tent and quickly go to fetch one, banishing the incident from my thoughts for now. I come back with two thin strips of wood. One to bind to the arm after straightening it, the other for the man to bite down on. I saw Father set broken bones many times and assisted him often.

"This is an ailment with which I will contend." I smile reassuringly at the man and give him the shorter of the sticks to place between his teeth. "This may hurt a little."

After countless wounds bathed in honey, bandages applied, limbs set, teeth examined, and incantations muttered, I rest my elbows on the mud bricks in a euphoric combination of exhaustion and delight.

Paser walks over, looking just as tired and just as happy. "A good day's work?"

"Yes." I grin up at him, my robes bloodied and vomit splattered. "You?"

"Excellent."

The sun has set and most of the people have gone back to their homes. We pack up our things. I shake my bag out and give it a quick wipe with one of the bandages, making sure there are no lingering internal organs. The busyness of the day caused me to forget the earlier gruesome discovery, but my thoughts are pulled back to wondering who might do such a thing. Paser notices the frown cross my face.

"What is it?" he asks.

"Somehow the contents of the nobleman's head from yesterday's demonstration ended up in my bag," I say, voice low. Or maybe it was his wife's.

Paser's eyes widen. "What?"

"See for yourself." I motion back toward a dust-covered lump on the ground.

"Why would someone do such a thing?" he asks.

"Perhaps someone is trying to discourage me from my studies," I say, thinking that is the most apt scenario. They will have to try a lot harder than that.

"Why?" Paser asks again.

"Maybe they do not think girls are meant to be doctors."

Paser scoffs. "That is nonsense. What about the Chief Physician Merit-Ptah? And the great Peseshet oversaw an entire body of female physicians."

"Still. There are many more examples of male doctors," I point out.

"Quantity is not always better than quality." He grins.

A laugh escapes. "A wise observation, Paser. You should inscribe that on a tomb somewhere, so it will be remembered."

"Maybe I will." He laughs along with me as Reb walks over.

"What is so funny?" he asks.

"Oh, nothing." I wave my hand casually but watch his face closely. "Someone just thought it would be funny to line my satchel with brain matter."

Reb visibly blanches. "Foul."

I want to make sure. "Did you do it, Reb?" I examine his expression for any sign, but there is none.

"We were just trying to figure out why a person would do such a thing," Paser says.

Reb hesitates.

"What?" My voice is as sharp as my scalpel. "Are you going to say it was because of my father?"

"It is a possibility," he says, meeting my eye.

"And what gives you cause to think such thoughts?" I demand.

"I have often heard my uncle discuss your father with some of the other High Priests," he informs me.

My eyes narrow. "What do they say?"

Reb glances around. "Perhaps we should talk about this somewhere else?"

I'm about to insist that here is as good a place as any, but Paser nods.

"He's right. Let's go."

We walk along the dusty path leading back to the temple. Paser and Reb talk about the last few hours' worth of work. I am silent. Reb has been nothing but antagonistic to me since my arrival. Can I even trust anything that comes from his mouth? His uncle, Nebifu, is also the Most High Priest and didn't get along with Father. Then again, that may be a reason to listen to Reb. Maybe he knows something and will let it slip.

We reach the temple and bow to the on-duty priests minding the entrance, walking past the giant statues guarding the front. The public is only allowed access to the temple during the holy festivals. This is sacred space.

"This way," Paser says, and I follow him, turning off one wing to reach a small room used for storing texts. I take a quick look around, but am sure this room would have been thoroughly searched, as well. The lights are dim, torches flickering. Pulling some reed mats into a circle, we sit, facing one another, shadows playing across our faces.

"So tell me, then," I say. "What do you know?"

"Your father was not the man you think he was, Sesha." Reb's tone is acerbic.

"And who exactly do *you* think he was?" I ask.

He looks down at the floor and back up again. "A heretic."

It is as if Reb has slapped me across the face. "No," I whisper.

That is the worst thing you can call somebody.

"Many did not agree with the recent changes he made to our learning here at the temple. My uncle said he did not give the gods proper credit for his work in healing. He became proud, referring to facts and new knowledge, disregarding some spells and incantations."

"My father was not a proud man," I say through clenched teeth. I do not believe Reb for a second.

"His dismissal of the gods angered the priests," Reb continues, "especially when Pharaoh remained unconcerned and instead brought him into the palace as a mark of honour. The priests were worried he would begin to hold sway over Pharaoh."

Thus lessening their own power. "So the priests had him killed?" I say, mouth dry. And maybe planted the insignia ring to fool anyone who found it?

"I do not know," Reb admits.

"Liar," I say.

He holds up his hands. "I swear to the gods. I have no reason to lie."

"What about your uncle?" My eyes narrow. "Don't you want to protect him?"

"Why would I do that?" he says. "Why do you think I told you all this, anyway?" His hand goes to a mark on his cheek, not quite faded, and his next few words are said simply. "I hate him."

"Why have you been so hostile?" I change the subject.

He shrugs. "I suppose some of my uncle's prejudices rubbed off on me. And it bothers me."

"What does?"

A wry look passes over his face. "That you show more talent as a physician than I ever will."

I look at him in disbelief. Those are the last words I'd ever expect to come from his mouth.

"Well, now." Paser smiles. "It only took you both the length of the Nile to get over yourselves."

After washing my face, I look around through squinted eyes for a dry towel.

"Here you are." One is thrust into my hands.

I blot my face and look up to see Kewat.

"Thanks to you," I say, voice cautious. "Are you well?"

"I did your test."

"And?"

"I am with child."

I am unsure whether she wishes a congratulations or not. Bebi flutters over.

"Did you ask her?" she demands.

"Not yet," Kewat says, eyeing me.

"Ask me what?" I say, getting the sense this conversation has happened before.

"Will you be my physician?" Kewat says.

"For the baby?" I ask in amazement.

"You have had much experience with your father. Everyone knows your skills as a midwife."

"I am not fully trained," I protest. "There are those more senior than me who would be a better choice …"

"I want you," Kewat says, brown eyes flashing. "It will not serve if my father discovers I am pregnant so soon and has the chance to interfere." She hesitates, then reaches her hands out and clasps mine between them. "Please, Sesha."

I look helplessly at Bebi, who shrugs a small shoulder.

"Very well," I say. "But if there are any complications, I am going to Ahmes."

"Thank you." Kewat emits a small glow and I wonder if it is the child already, lighting her from within. Lucky for her she does not seem to be suffering from any of the sickness that usually accompanies early pregnancy. My mother said she had thrown up her morning meal every day for nine full moons with both Ky and me.

Going to my bed, my eye is caught by the wooden box and I take out the scroll Merat gave me in thanks the other night. The few girls that notice pay no attention, not having much of an interest in something they are unable to do. Maybe I will start a small class to teach any who want to learn. Scanning the document, I marvel at the delicate papyrus. Never have I seen it pounded so thin. Almost translucent. It appears to be a journal of some sort, containing various incantations and prayers, many of which I am unable to read due to the sophisticated glyphs. The recordings of a high-ranking scribe.

A name at the bottom of the document captures my attention.

Qar.

Something clicks. That was the name of the priest who originally found the missing scroll. The one who died just after my parents. Wujat said his illness was most sudden. Though death comes swiftly here, it seems highly coincidental that both men who handled the scroll are now gone. I wonder how this particular document ended up in Merat's possession? Perhaps some of his things came into the palace with Wujat?

"Sesha." It is Bebi. She settles under her blanket and I put the papyrus aside. "Thank you for helping Kewat. It is most kind of you. Especially because of the way she treated you."

"It is my duty," I say. "There is an oath upon the physician."

"Have you sworn your oaths yet?"

"Not yet," I admit. "But that does not mean I do not abide by them."

"Well" — Bebi yawns — "it is kind of you all the same." She looks at me and sighs. "Kewat is my cousin.

Not my favourite, but still family. It is a risk she takes, one I advised against, but she has never listened to anyone but herself."

"You never mentioned she was your cousin," I say.

"I wanted you to like me," Bebi confides.

I smile. "I do not hold the character of people's family members against them."

"There are many who do." Bebi yawns again sleepily. "Good night, Sesha."

"Good night, Bebi."

I lie there awake for a while, pondering her words. Perhaps one of the scribes holds my father against me. Maybe it was one of the priests who put the brains in my satchel. Logic suggests it was someone from the temple, someone who had access. It also could have been meant to frighten me from my quest. Though the only people who know of that are the ones who wish the scroll to be found almost as much as I do. Not that that is a reason to trust anyone at the palace. Sighing, I add another item to my ever-growing list of things to uncover and then feel myself surrender to sleep.

24

"**W**AKE UP!"

My eyes fly open and I sit up in alarm. "What is it? Has something happened?"

Ky stands over my bed. "It is Festival Eve!"

I groan and pull my blanket back over my head. "Please, Ky, just a few more moments of sleep." The week has been filled with non-stop lessons and ceaseless hunting for the scroll, while trying to work out exactly what is going on. In addition to treating and diagnosing patients and teaching Merat to read, somehow I have been designated as unofficial physician to all of the handmaidens. Since I agreed to be Kewat's doctor, the women have been coming to me with endless health questions.

"Come on!" The blanket is ripped off and one of my eyelids peels itself back to glare at my brother, who despite his recent setback, has been the picture of health this past week. I am not fooled though. I know the sickness is there, lurking, waiting for the moment we drop our guard to show itself. My exhaustion is replaced with newfound vigour. If Ky can manage to be this cheerful this early in the morning, so can I.

"All right, I am coming," I say, sitting up and yawning.

The other handmaidens pat him on the head, murmuring their hellos as I get ready for temple. Accepting their attentions good-naturedly, he waits for me outside the room.

"Sesha, what is that remedy, again?" one of the older handmaidens inquires as she passes, itching at a large red patch on her arm.

"Grind up some grapes into a fine paste and mix them with honey or the juice of the aloe vera plant, adding a few drops of castor oil," I recite. "Apply it to the skin and leave on overnight. That should relieve most of the irritation. And try not to scratch!"

"Thank you," she singsongs, ruffling my hair, which I tie back for the day's work. In my studies, and tending people who need help, it is easy to see the results of my actions. Not as satisfying is scouring the temple, eavesdropping on fellow priests and scribes, and avoiding Wujat and Pharaoh's persistent inquiries into how my search is going.

I join Ky in the hall. "Hello, little brother." Someone is excited for the festival. Lasting four moons, the Inundation is a time for great revelry and celebrating. At its beginning, the gods are beseeched if the Nile's waters are too low or too high. Isis shines bright in the evening sky, heralding the oncoming floods, when her tears for her dead husband, Osiris, cover the land. We are now finishing the second month, which is marked by the festival. A month and half after my parents died. A half-moon's worth of days at the palace and despite all my best efforts, the scroll remains unfound.

"You have been busy, Sister?" Ky asks.

"Some of us are not free to play all day, stuffing our faces with food and drink while finding new and wicked ways to entertain ourselves," I say with mock seriousness.

He laughs and pats his stomach. "I have almost forgotten what it feels like to be hungry." His smile fades slightly. "Almost."

"You are safe now, Brother," I say softly. Or for the moment at least. Despite the unfruitfulness of my search, the last week has lulled me into feeling secure, as well; the busy routines of my days and evenings a temporary gauze on the wound my parents' death tore across my heart. And though I know the sensation of well-being is only a mirage, it is a constant struggle to resist the hypnotism of daily palace life. I cannot let myself be charmed and must remain vigilant in my search, on guard for predators. I know now how Apep must have felt. "What are your plans for the day?" I ask. Not being able to see him much as of late, I asked Ahmes if he might excuse Ky from his morning's duties so we could break the fast together.

We sneak into the kitchens and Cook parcels us out some food. Taking it into the sunny courtyard we go sit by the pond. Merat often watches the fish in it swim, bright shapes darting back and forth. She says it relaxes her. Ky watches them for a moment as I methodically massage my pomegranate to release its juices, my thumbs pushing firmly into the round fruit, feeling the burst of seeds under its skin.

"I have heard things of our father," he finally says over the rhythmic crunching, shattering the tranquility of the morning.

I was wondering when he would, knowing how gossip spreads at the palace. It was always a matter of when and not if. I take a small bite of the pomegranate, spit out the rind and bring the fruit to my lips, tilting my head back so the sweet juice runs down my throat. "What have you heard?" Wiping my chin, I keep my voice as level as the stones that form the Great Pyramid.

"That he was a heretic." Ky's own voice cracks. "That he did not believe in the gods and their magic."

"He was no such thing, Ky." I take a breath and offer him the fruit to drink. "Father talked often of magic. He believed it connected everyone and everything. But he also believed in things like medicine, herbology, mathematics, astronomy, and logic. And that one did not diminish the other, but rather that they were entwined with another. Inseparable."

Ky lets out a huge sigh and hands me back the fruit. "I know. But it still feels good to hear you say it."

He gives a wistful smile, his lips red from the juice of the pomegranate. "I just wanted to speak with some-one about it."

"You may always speak of them to me," I say. "After all, that is how we remember them."

And to an Egyptian, there is nothing more import-ant than being remembered.

The temple is a sandstorm of frenetic activity. Junior scribes rush about, completing errands and chores. The more senior scribes and priests generally look har-ried and bark at anyone appearing idle.

"Tomorrow is our best chance," I say in a low voice to Paser and Reb at the midday meal.

"When?" Paser asks.

"During the procession." The priests will parade the statue of the god Amun through the streets with thousands of people jostling to catch a glimpse before it is taken into the temple. Hundreds of servants and junior scribes will wave palm fronds while people sing, cheer, and make merry. Other priests and scribes will be busy taking offerings and giving out vast quantities of food and drink to be consumed as people celebrate late into the night and right on through to the next day.

"What is your plan?" Reb says. Though I still do not trust him completely, his help will be welcome.

"If you keep watch at the entrance to the temple, Paser and I can search the places where we have not had a chance to look," I say. "Once the High Priests arrive with the statue, you will bang the gong three times to signal that the ceremony is about to begin."

Reb is skeptical. "What about the priests who remain here with the king and queen? They will be waiting to greet the statue of the god and present their gifts."

"That is where Merat comes in," I say.

"Merat?" Paser looks up. "What does she have to do with this?"

"If anyone sees anything they shouldn't, she is going to cause a distraction," I say. I spoke with the princess at our last lesson. She knows that I have been charged by her father and Wujat to find the scroll. I explained that the priests were most particular about their documents and it would be best if I did not have to worry about them impeding my search. She happily agreed to provide a diversion. Especially upon hearing of Paser's involvement.

"I do not understand," Reb says. "If Pharaoh and Wujat asked you to find the scroll, then why do you care about the other priests knowing?"

"They asked for my discretion," I say. What I told Merat is true. The higher scribes will not take kindly to a lowly junior scribe — the daughter of one who appeared to have fallen from grace, no less — riffling their sanctuary, going through their valuable and historical documents. In addition, Pharaoh, and to some extent Wujat, are the most powerful men in the land and part of their power comes from keeping those happy who also possess some power themselves, no matter how small. For in discontent lies potential for plots and scheming. Pharaoh reaffirmed the last time we talked that with all of the external threats, he does not need to be concerned about internal ones as well just now. Things were becoming increasingly unstable with the Hyksos in the North. Only a few days ago a suspected spy was captured and interrogated.

Reb gets up to help himself to another portion of food. Speaking of discontent, I hope there will be enough refreshment to go around during the festival. I offer up a quick prayer for a good harvest.

"And you are at peace with doing their bidding?" Paser's voice is as quiet as moth wings once Reb leaves. He knows how conflicted I am, wondering whether someone at the palace could possibly be involved with the fire.

"Do I really have a choice?" I say. Not only will finding the scroll save thousands of lives — not least of all my brother's — but it might also provide some answers to that night.

I have yet to mention the ring to Ky, having been so busy and not wanting to trouble him over something that may turn out to be nothing. And there is his friendship with Tutan to consider. Pharaoh and his family treat Ky as a son and it will trouble his spirit greatly to have any potential evidence of their involvement. My spirit, however, has been much tempered these past few moons; it has become as strong as metal.

"You will be careful?" Paser asks, with that direct expression he has. The one that looks like he can see right into me.

"I will," I say, mouth feeling oddly dry. I take a sip of my drink. "And you, as well?" It is fortuitous that Paser has a taste for intrigue and adventure, in addition to being a good person.

"Sesha, I —"

Just then Reb comes back with a full plate. "What did I miss?"

"I was just telling Sesha to be careful," Paser says, taking a roll from Reb's plate. "Now, let's discuss the remaining spots where the scroll could be hidden."

As Paser and Reb debate whether the innermost sanctuary is a likely hiding place, I wonder at what Paser was about to divulge. A warning? Or some other kind of revelation? Tamping down my curiosity, I focus on the task at hand. Today is a big day and may very well be our best chance to find the scroll. We have been through the temple with one of Nebet's fine-toothed combs and there are only a few areas we've not been able to access, the underground catacombs in particular. All my focus and determination must be put to the task at hand. I think of Ky, Merat, my parents, and the safety of the whole kingdom. The stakes are much too great to fail now.

25

THE DAY PASSES IN A BLUR. The Most High Priests left yesterday to retrieve the statue of the god from the neighbouring temple. It is being brought up the river on the pharaoh's royal ship. People have lined the banks and the majority of the priests and scribes wait down at the docks. Cheers and singing float toward the temple on the wind. The statue will be placed on a smaller boat made entirely of gold and silver, inlaid with amethyst and turquoise. The boat bearing the statue will then be placed on a wooden platform and carried by the scribes up through the crowds, along the path, between the avenue of Sphinxes, and, finally, to the towering entrance of the temple.

That is when Reb will sound the gong and Paser and I will know to sneak back out into the fray before anyone finds us nosing around where no junior scribe should be. The temple is nearly deserted. Pharaoh and

Queen Anat, along with Tabira, Merat, and Tutan, who looks bored, wait in the main room with their personal attendants, musicians, and a few of the higher-level priests, snacking, drinking and chatting among themselves.

A few of Pharaoh's personal guards stand by the entrance to the temple, their firm stance reminiscent of the giant statues guarding the front of the holy structure. Piles of tributes for the gods lie beside the elaborate three-tiered platform the royals sit on. Ky is there, looking as bored as Tutan. I can tell the boys have been placed under stern orders to behave. He looks around for me but I remain hidden. Ky is the one person I have never been able to tell untruths to, and I know he will see immediately in my face that we are up to something. Just then Paser catches my eye and gives me a quick nod.

Time to go.

We mapped out the temple with sticks in the sand. Paser will take the west wing and I will take the east. Both lead down into their own separate labyrinths and meet somewhere in the middle. Access to the labyrinths is usually strictly monitored, but all hands are needed for the ceremony. This is our opportunity to delve into places forbidden to all but the most senior priests.

Moving quickly, I keep my eyes down, careful not to attract any attention. Paser gave Reb and me a brief lesson in defence the other day, in case we should have need of it. Most priests are not violent, but there is always the chance that one of them might react unfavourably to any unsanctioned behaviour. And they will not hesitate to beat a junior scribe. I remember the look in Reb's eyes — he knows that all too well.

Wincing, I rub the large purple and blue mark on my upper arm, a token of our training session. Though my month outside the palace taught me much, I survived mostly by being quick and clever, not by taking the offensive. Paser's teachings affirmed my methods. He told us when our opponent strikes first, we must duck away and then, when they are off balance, attack.

"If you are not strong, then you must be smart," he said. "And if you are not smart, then you must be strong."

"And if you are both?" Reb asked, voice full of bravado.

"Then you have nothing to fear, my friend." Paser laughed and clapped him on the back.

I did not ask the question I have been wrestling with of late, not wanting to appear weak in front of either of them. But I could not help thinking it all the same: "What if you are neither?"

Now is not the time for self-doubt, Sesha. You survived a moon on your own with your brother to care for.

You are on the path to finding the scroll and saving him. Have hope.

The voice whispers to me now, not spoken but rather felt, as the torches lighting the dim hallway flicker.

I take a few deep breaths to calm my racing heart. *All right, Father. Where did you hide the scroll?*

There is no answer and I am left again to my own devices. Father always did say you learn more by doing. But after I go in and out of several rooms of the east wing, nothing jumps out at me as to where the document might be hidden. I sigh. Searching for a scroll in the temple is like searching for a scarab in the desert. Unless it chooses to reveal itself, it will remain unseen.

The sound of footsteps stops me in my tracks.

Flattening myself against the cold stone walls, I hold my breath, praying to the gods the footsteps do not round the corner.

Closer and closer they come. Desperately, I look around for somewhere, anywhere, I can hide. This time there is nothing.

Whoever it is rounds the corner and I feel the air leave my lungs in a *whoosh*.

Paser.

"You scared the ankh out of me," I hiss, much relieved it is him.

"Come on, you have to see this." He gestures with the torch in his hand and I follow him down the dark hallway, deeper into the earth. The air is much cooler down here.

As Paser leads me through the dizzying maze, turning this way and that, a question I have been wanting to ask bursts forth. "Earlier, you were about to say something before Reb joined us," I say. "Do you mind telling me now?"

He sighs, his breath causing the torch to flicker. "I learned who left the brains in your bag."

"Who?"

"It was Djaty." Paser names the boy who fainted during the mummification procedure and then again at the snake.

"Why?" I ask, bewildered.

"He was embarrassed at being ... overcome in front of everyone. I supposed he thought it would be a way to earn back respect from the others."

It is my turn to huff, almost blowing out my torch. Boys. Though I am relieved it was meant as a harmless prank and not something more insidious.

We take note of our turns, at last coming to a small chamber.

"In here," Paser says.

We walk into the room. It is dark and I do not see what is so special about it. There are a few objects lying around, some older garments of the priests heaped in a pile.

"What is it?" I ask.

"Stand still," he says. "Close your eyes."

I obey and we stand there in silence for a few moments.

"I do not —"

"Sssh," he says, "do you hear that?"

I try to listen for something, and then I hear it. A soft whistling sound.

I open my eyes. "What is it?"

"A breeze," he says. "Somewhere there is air flowing through here."

I close my eyes again. "I hear it. And it feels warm."

We walk around the room, holding our torches aloft, searching for the source of the balmy wind.

The light is so dim it is difficult to see. Closing my eyes, I touch my hand to the stone wall. Slowly, I trace my way around the room, using all my senses. I reach a spot where the air feels warmer.

"Here," I whisper, opening my eyes. I begin to press against the large stone bricks making up the wall, Paser doing the same.

Nothing.

After a few minutes of this, I slump to the ground, unsuccessful. Paser comes and sits beside me.

"We are fooling ourselves. The scroll will never be found!" I say, slamming my back hard against the stone.

Something shifts behind me. "Did you feel that?" I am unsure if I imagined the subtle movement of the stone.

Paser quickly spins on his bottom and braces his feet against the block in the wall. He pushes with all his strength and it moves back a few cubits.

"Sesha, help me!"

I turn around and put my feet on the stone, bracing my body with my hands pressed firmly into the dirt floor.

"One, two, three," Paser says. We push our soles against the stone and it scrapes back in protest. The air flows in warmer now.

Paser looks at me. "Once more?"

I nod. Grunting, we push with all our strength. My hands slip in the dirt and I dig my nails into the hard ground. At last the stone slides all the way back, leaving enough room for a body to slip through.

Panting, Paser shines his torch into the dark space we've opened up. "After you."

Crawling on my hands and knees and keeping my head low, I pass through thick solid stones on both sides and above me, pushing my shoulder hard into the shifted stone to create a little more space, then I wiggle my body through.

It is as black as a night without stars. I turn and reach my arm back into the square stone passageway to grab the torch from Paser. He crawls through, one hand holding the flame aloft, and passes it to me, then reverses and grabs the other one. He crawls through the narrow space again and passes the second one to me. Now holding both torches, I back out of the way and stand up, casting my light around what appears to be a very large chamber.

Lifting the torches up even higher in wonder, I gasp. The room is piled high with glittering treasures beyond imagining. Enormous solid gold statues, sparkling jewels and shimmering gemstones, gleaming silver, and ancient artifacts fill the cavernous space, making the nobleman's items seem like a drop in a reed bucket. Paser stands up beside me, brushing himself off, and gives a low whistle as I pass him a torch.

"What do you think it is all doing here?" I ask in awe, casting the flame around to light up the corners of the chamber.

"Maybe it is a secret treasury of the temple?" Paser walks around, lightly touching a priceless object here, examining an artifact there. Slowly, we make our way to the back of the room in astonishment. Finally, my eyes set upon the most astonishing thing of all: dozens of wooden shelves line one wall, stacked with hundreds and thousands of scrolls, neatly rolled into thin cylinders.

My scribe's heart beats faster at the sight of so many in one place, but at the same time it sinks at the sheer number of them.

"Do you think it is in there?" Paser whispers.

Biting my lip, I contemplate the question. "I am not sure." It does seem like a perfect location to keep the papyrus: safe and away from prying eyes. But if Father was immersed in transcribing the scroll, he would want it more accessible. "It is likely the place where the original document was found."

"It certainly is private," Paser echoes my thoughts as he walks behind an enormous quartzite statue of Hathor, the cow goddess. The sun resting between her golden horns is made of pure gold, the horns themselves a lustrous silver. He disappears from view behind another towering statue. It is of the Great Imhotep himself.

I stare up at the face of the legendary doctor and priest, one of the most revered men in our history. Imhotep was a scribe, like me, as well as Grand Vizier and adviser to several kings. He was also an astrologer, a poet, a sage, and a revolutionary architect. It was he who designed and built the very first step pyramid for King Djoser, creating the model that inspired the Great Pyramids — a lasting contribution to our nation's legacy. I think of civilizations to come who will marvel at the awe-inspiring structures, and wonder what they will be like. It is also for them that we must preserve the scroll, so that they may learn from us.

"Sesha!" Paser calls from behind the statue. "There is a writing table here. And some documents drawn up in a fine hand."

Hurrying over to the table, I bring my torch, illuminating papyri containing flowing hieratic script. My heartbeat roars in my ears like the mighty lion. Swallowing, I look from the writing to Paser.

"These are written in my father's hand."

26

WE SIFT THROUGH THE PAPERS.

"Look for anything that resembles a medical document," I say, holding the torch closer. The roaring in my ears has faded somewhat, but handling manuscripts my father actually composed is having an effect on me.

"Oh, really? I thought to keep an eye out for a collection of poems." I do not miss the teasing in Paser's voice.

"Merat also talked of poems," I say, examining one of the documents up close.

"What did she say?"

"It is why she wants to learn to read and write. So she may compose them." I put the document down; it is not what we are looking for. Turning, I glance around the area. "It has to be here."

"Sesha." Paser's voice is not teasing anymore.

"Yes?"

"Why do you think your father went to such lengths to keep the scroll hidden from the other priests?"

I say the only thing that comes to mind. "Maybe he was afraid they would destroy it before he had a chance to finish copying it."

"Why would they do that?" Paser asks.

"I suppose we will know the answer to that when we find the scroll."

Dong. A faint reverberation sounds through the air.

"It's Reb," Paser says. "The procession must be arriving at the temple."

"Hurry!" I say, picking up various scraps of papyrus and frantically scanning them.

Dong.

In my haste, I drop my torch to the ground. Quickly crouching to pick it up before it is snuffed out, my eyes go to underneath the desk, where the dying flames show something.

"Paser, bring your light! There is something under here."

Paser shines his light under the desk. As I reach for the papyrus, I know this is it.

Dong.

"Sesha, we must go!" Paser urges.

There is no time to make sure. Grabbing the scroll, I stand up, leaving my dead torch on the ground. We run the length of the room, sidestepping and darting around magnificent treasures and silent statues until we reach the pushed-aside stone block.

Dropping to my hands and knees I crawl through first, Paser right behind me. Or at least I think he's right behind me. Looking over my shoulder, I see that the space I just wiggled myself through is empty.

"Paser!" I panic.

"Coming." His torch winks out and he drops to his knees. Once he is through he stands and takes off the belt holding up his kilt. I stare in confusion as he tucks one end of his skirt tightly into the other, ducks down, and crawls back through the passageway. He backs out again, grunting with effort, and I realize he has looped his belt around the stone and is dragging it into place.

"Give me an end!" I say and he passes me the thin cord. We pull the block with all our might, bodies straining until it reluctantly slides into place. Paser whips out the belt and wraps it around his waist again. I spot something else tucked into his skirt but there is no time for questions. We stand and run down the corridor, retracing our steps until at last we emerge from the bowels of the temple, winded and panting. Tucking the scroll inside my robe, I make an effort to stop gasping and stand up straight. Paser does the same, and as he does, floats something light and gauzy around my shoulders.

"The scroll isn't exactly entirely unnoticeable." He puffs. "This will help conceal it."

"Where did you get it?" I finger the delicate fabric. There is no doubt that a garment this fine belonged to a queen.

"It was hanging off one of the statues."

I shake out a sleepy scorpion, then wrap the shawl tightly over my shoulders, tying it in front of my body to cover the cylindrical outline of the scroll. We attempt to stroll leisurely back down the main halls, to where we can blend in with the rest of the scribes.

"You, there!"

A sharp voice freezes us in mid-step. Slowly, we turn. I paste on an innocent expression and pull the shawl tighter, hoping no one will notice its quality.

Sebau strides over to us. "Why are you not with the others?" He eyes us suspiciously.

"We went to get more incense for one of the other priests," Paser says without hesitation.

"Where is it?" Sebau demands, impatient as always.

"Um, we are all out," I say.

"That cannot be!" Sebau looks panicked. "I myself supervised the ordering." Muttering to himself he marches off, presumably in the direction of the incense stocks.

We both slump in relief.

"What do you think he will do when he sees there is plenty of incense left?" I ask Paser.

"Think we are idiots for not looking in the right place," Paser says, grinning.

I let out a loud laugh, releasing nerves and tension. It echoes down the hall and two priests carrying baskets of offerings give us a disapproving look.

My whole body is tingling, electrified at the thought that the scroll in my robes could actually be the one we've been searching for.

"Come on, let's go to the main chamber. Reb will be wondering if we made it without getting caught."

Still feeling giddy from our narrow escape, I nudge Paser with my elbow. "It is a good thing you did not have to use your defensive moves on Sebau. I have a feeling he would be most put out at our next class."

"I would be the one put out," Paser laughs as we walk down the hall. "Cast out in the desert to shrivel like a grape left in the sun."

A thought occurs to me. "Where did you learn to fight?" I am curious about Paser's background. Aside from mentioning that he, too, lost his parents, I realize I know little about him.

"My mother's father," he says. "He was a soldier in the pharaoh's army." I recall Merat mentioning the general. Paser continues, "He thought I spent too much time studying and decided he would train me to defend myself. As he cared for me since I was six, I learned much."

"You did not want to follow in his footsteps?"

"I wanted to be a scribe, like my father before me," he says. "I have a love for the written word and it is my belief that more effective fighting can be done with scripts than weapons. Still, I did enjoy my training." He mock flexes his muscles, which are remarkably well-developed considering his chosen profession. "And both have their benefits."

I laugh again as we enter the main chamber. The roar of the crowds is loud and the room is full of priests, scribes, and the royal family and their entourage, all looking very grand and regal.

"How will we find Reb?" I ask.

"Don't worry," says Paser. "He will find us."

We make our way toward the raised platform where Pharaoh is preparing to officially receive the statue before it is taken to the inner sanctuary. Priestesses from another temple chant and sing sacred hymns, rattling their *sistrums*. The statue will remain covered until that final moment when it is revealed to those fortunate enough to be present, who will behold its greatness. It is believed that the spirit of the gods dwells within their statues and within our pharaoh.

Wujat and Nebifu walk the revered statue up to Pharaoh and Queen Anat, each firmly holding a side of the small silver table it rests upon.

Merat catches my eye and I give her a brief nod to let her know that all is well. Her distraction will not be needed. I do not miss the flash of disappointment that crosses her face and lower my head to hide a smile.

Pharaoh's voice booms loud through the chamber. "The gods have blessed us and *Kemut*, this black and fertile land we live upon." Relief spreads through my body; the harvest is expected to be bountiful then. Pharaoh holds up his hands in a wide gesture. "They are most pleased at their servants' work." He gives a respectful nod to the priests closest to the platform and places a hand over the beautifully embroidered shroud covering the statue. "Tonight we will celebrate their pleasure and take our own, rejoicing together as one." He whips the shroud off the statue with a flourish as loud cheers erupt in the room. It is smaller than I imagined, especially after the treasures I just had at my fingertips, but no less impressive; polished gold and silver gleam in the sun's rays shining though the temple. Those outside the temple walls hear the deafening hails and praises for the king and let out their own raucous cries, not needing to hear the exact words to recognize the sentiment.

After several moments Queen Anat takes one end of the shroud that Pharaoh still holds, and they drape it gracefully back over the statue. She then steps forward and raises her arms high. "Bow before your king, Almighty Pharaoh, Lord of all the Lands, and the gods' representative deity on earth! He, who maintains *Ma'at*, universal harmony, and direct interpreter of the gods' will. Bow down before him!"

Everyone in the room obliges, dropping to their knees, hands raised. The gong is sounded so those outside the temple for miles around know to do the same as we bask in the greatness of the gods. The gong is sounded again and we rise, chanting the sacred vowels. Bumps prickle my flesh at the sounds. Gongs and the intonation of certain vowels have magical powers, believed to promote strength and good health. Father used both often in his healing. He thought that the sounds resonated through our bodies and infiltrated organisms too small to even see, flushing out sickness and promoting wellness.

The procession makes its final leg of the journey to the inner sanctuary. Wujat and Nebifu carry the covered statue, and Pharaoh and his family follow them down the platform. Two more High Priests make up the final members of the most privileged family of the lands. As the last of the entourage walks down the hallway, Nebifu, High Priest of the Temple, rather anticlimactically, takes the stage. He lifts his arms wide as Queen Anat did and though he lacks her sheer presence, his words are greeted with just as much reverence.

"Let the festivities begin!"

27

"DID YOU GET IT?"

Reb appears at our side. The party is under way. Drinks are overflowing and celebrants descend like locusts on the mouth-watering food being brought in. I suppose there is no need to be conservative with provisions now. The palace is full to the rooftops, playing host to elite guests from all over the land. A few of the younger scribes, the lowest level admitted to the party, are over in the corner. Some play games of Senet, and Hounds and Jackals. Others draw pictures of the sparsely clothed dancing girls, the lively trio across the way playing the lute, lyre, and zither, and the acrobats flying through the air — recording the festival for posterity. Tabira runs by pulling her wooden donkey and shrieking with laughter, her nurse chasing her.

"Let's go outside and talk." The scroll presses against my ribcage and I fight the urge to rip it from my robes to examine it. The room is warm from all the people and I also do not want my sweat blurring the ink. We head to the large outdoor courtyard with the pool. The night air is fragrant with the perfumes of the flowers people wear around their necks.

There is more music out here; contortionists manipulate their arms, legs, and spines into twisted shapes, defying the skeletal system. Singers hammer the drums as people gyrate, their bodies interpreters for the beat.

"Over there." Paser nods at a slightly less occupied corner of the courtyard and we walk. Parched, I grab a glass of something off a tray being carried by another scribe. He gives me a look like he has stepped in donkey dung.

"My most humble thanks." I raise my glass to him, unable to control my euphoria.

"Do you have it?" Reb repeats.

"Shh," I say, taking a drink. "Ky!" I spot my brother with Tutan, the pair throwing a ball back and forth between them. He gives me a wave but does not come over. It must be a serious game of catch.

I walk toward the garden, wanting the lush blooms and tall palms for their privacy. Ducking behind a large tree with a thick base, I finish the rest of my drink, which is overly sweet and warm. Paser and Reb join me. After making sure we are alone, I reach my hand underneath the shawl and into my robes, pulling out the papyrus with as much flourish as Pharaoh.

"Do you think that is really it?" Paser asks, glancing around over his shoulders.

"There is only one way to find out." Ever so gently, I begin to unwind the scroll. "Wait." I stop, my eagerness is making me careless. "Perhaps we should be doing this somewhere a little more … secure."

"Where do you suggest?" Reb is impatient.

An idea comes to me. "What about Ahmes's private quarters? He will be set up in the medical ward with some of the other doctors." Inevitably, there are a lot of injuries at a celebration of this size. And it seems fitting that we open the scroll with some of my father's things around us.

"He's probably wondering where we are," Paser says. "The junior scribes are on shifts to help out in the infirmary."

"This is yet another disadvantage of being a scribe," Reb grumbles. "We do not even get to fully enjoy the celebrations."

"The runts of the litter often get the least to eat and drink," Paser says, grinning.

"I told him we would do a later shift," I say, tucking the scroll back into my robe.

"Good thinking," Paser says.

I know how to get to my father's old chambers from any spot in the palace and we make our way there now. People are becoming increasingly more festive and we have to dodge around some of the more zealous revellers.

"Sesha." We almost bump into Merat. "It seems you did not need my services after all."

"Your Highness was most gracious in her offer," I say. *Please let her be on her way. Please let her be on her way.* I like Merat well, but she is the pharaoh's daughter and I need some time with the scroll before he finds out we have it.

"Where are you three going?" she asks, lifting an imperious eyebrow.

"Um, um …" I stammer, trying to come up with a suitable foil, but the drink has slightly dimmed my thought processes. *For the love of Isis!*

Reb is no better; not used to speaking with a princess, he stands there frozen, like a hyena caught in the light of a torch, mouth dementedly agape.

"Ah, then. Intrigue." She crosses her arms. "Lead on, I will accompany you." With no choice, we resume our pace and she walks with us, at the front.

"Has Your Highness been enjoying the festivities?" Paser moves beside her, as Reb and I follow close behind.

"Not as much as some people." She nods at a group of people dancing and laughing. "How can I, when my father is about to announce my fate, one that will send me away from my home forever?"

"See, Reb?" I mutter under my breath. "Royal life is not all riches and parties."

"Does Your Highness mind sharing her announcement with us?" Paser asks.

I have not said anything to Paser of Merat's engagement, not wanting to betray the princess's confidence, but also not wanting to shake his focus from our search.

"It is not *my* announcement," she says. "But I am to be married." She gives him a sideways glance. "To a boorish Hyksos chieftain twice my age, as a gesture of goodwill." I do not miss the desolation in her voice. "Did Sesha not tell you?"

"No," Paser says, looking back over his shoulder at me. "She did not." Time enough to soothe Paser's feelings later. We reach the wing leading to the physician's chambers. Motioning for the others to stop, I peek my head around the corner. The way is clear.

"So what is it we are doing?" Merat whispers as we scurry down the hall, furtive as palace mice.

"Looking at something," I murmur as we reach the door to the chamber. Cautiously, I push it open. There are a few torches burning low; they will not last long.

Walking over to the long wooden counter, I pull the scroll from my robes and again, with extreme care, begin to unroll it. As it unfurls, I realize it is actually a scroll within a scroll. The inner one is much, much older than the outer papyrus. The hand of the faded papyrus is in the older style, and almost unreadable, though immaculate in its script.

It bears the cartouche of the Great Imhotep.

The newer scroll is a replica of the first, though the paper is much fresher and the hand is more familiar.

My father's.

I quickly scan the document, and the medical language leaps out at me as do the case numbers of each ailment. Blinking, I bite my lip to keep from shouting out.

The scrolls have been found at last.

"Is it what you have been seeking, Sesha?" Paser asks as the torches flicker and sputter.

"Yes." I force myself to breathe.

"And what is that?" Our heads whip around in unison as a bright glare shines in from the doorway, emblazoning Ahmes's frame.

28

AHMES WALKS INTO THE ROOM.

"What are you doing here?" I ask.

"I came to get some more medicines," he says. Coming closer, he shines his light on us. "More pertinently, what are your reasons for being in my chambers? And unauthorized, I might add."

Taking a deep breath, I decide to tell him. He must be the one to operate on Ky anyway. "We have found the scroll."

"The ancient medical papyrus?" Disbelief rings in his voice as he quickly approaches the workbench. The others move aside to make a space for him. Staring down at the ancient papyrus and its fresher brother, he examines it with care and veneration, careful not to touch the archaic script.

"I do not believe it." The excitement of a passionate scholar and physician is apparent. "Where did you find it?"

I hesitate. Another thought has been occurring to me, one sparked by Paser's question about why my father went to such lengths to hide the scroll: what was he doing in a room full of unimaginable treasures? There is no way he was involved in secreting them away.

Is there?

"They were in my quarters." Merat flicks her hair over her shoulder. "Sesha has been teaching me to read and, unthinkingly, I took some documents from the temple to practise with. I did not realize the significance of this particular scroll."

Ahmes looks as though he does not believe her, but one does not contradict the princess.

"Ahmes," I urge, "now that we have the scroll, you can do the surgery on Ky."

"Sesha, you must give this to the pharaoh at once," he counters.

"No!" I half shout, then lower my voice. If there is a war to come, there will be chaos. If it's critical to the campaign, there is no telling if I will ever see the scroll again once I let it go. "First you do the surgery, then I will give it to Pharaoh." I send both him and Merat a desperate look, pleading with them to understand. "My brother is all I have left in this world. You must do the surgery. You must."

Ahmes looks torn. He knows there may be retribution if Pharaoh and Wujat find out we have the scroll and did not tell them. "Sesha, I —"

My body shudders violently, as if I have taken an infusion of castor oil. I open my mouth to protest when Merat speaks.

"You will do the surgery, Ahmes," she commands. "My father and Wujat have waited this long for the papyrus. Another day or two will not harm them any."

He nods slowly, reluctant but acquiescent. And for the second time in as many minutes, I am glad that one does not contradict the princess.

Decision made, the details are dispatched with efficiency. Ahmes will do the surgery in two days' time. Reb and Paser are to assist. Ahmes says I am not allowed because I will not be able to remain detached enough to be useful.

"I will wait with you, Sesha," Merat says, after I unsuccessfully try to change Ahmes's mind. "We will not leave the room."

"Thank you, Your Highness," I say as we reach the main courtyard. I must find Ky to tell him the news. Then I will meet Ahmes and the others back at the main infirmary to help with the sick and injured from the party.

"Merat, there you are, my daughter." Queen Anat descends on us, looking especially striking this evening. Her glittering eyes are boldly outlined in a most becoming shade of malachite, her lips and cheeks artfully stained with red ochre. Stylish henna covers her arms and hands.

I bow low. "Your Majesty."

She inclines her head at me but speaks to Merat. "Your father is looking for you. He wishes to reveal the exalted news of your upcoming marriage."

Merat's jaw tightens. "Sorry, Mother, I needed a bit of fresh air. Sesha was just keeping me company."

The queen turns and examines me. "Sesha, what a lovely scarf you have on." She fingers the superior fabric. "Where in the heavens did you come across it?"

"It, uh, was my mother's," I say.

"It did not perish in the fire?" She lifts an eyebrow, an exact replica of her daughter.

"No … I … I found it here, in my father's, I mean, Ahmes's quarters. It was … uh … a gift for my mother to mark their fifteenth year together. Father must have accepted it from one of the nobles, in return for his services."

"Ah," she says, dismissing it and me. "Come, Merat, you have kept your father long enough."

They float off, leaving me flushed and shaky.

"Sesha!"

"Ky! There you are. I have been looking for you." Anubis barks in greeting and I scratch his head. "Where is Tutan?"

"His father is making some kind of announcement. He said I did not have to go with him." Ky seems happy to be momentarily relieved of his duties.

"Most magnanimous of him." I smile. "I have wonderful news." Glancing around to ensure no one is listening, I lower my voice. "We have found the scroll."

"The one Father was working on?" A myriad of emotions crosses his face.

"Yes! And that is not all. Ahmes is going to perform the surgery on you in two days' time!"

Ky's hand goes to Anubis. "Oh."

"Is that all you can say? This is wonderful news!"

Ky shrugs. "I … am not sure I want it."

"What?" I am stunned. "Ky, what are you saying? This may save your life."

"If it is the gods' will that I have this sickness, then so be it." He gnaws on his lower lip.

Seeing the fear in his eyes, my voice softens. "Ky, all will be well. Ahmes is going to study the document pertaining to your case. It was written by the Great Imhotep himself. And I will be there, for every drop of water to fall from the water clock."

"Where did you find the scroll?" Ky asks, changing the subject.

"In the temple. In a room —" I cut myself off. Ky is still young and may accidentally reveal to Tutan the location of the secret room. Before that happens I want to figure out what Father was doing in a room full of treasure that no one else seems to know about. I know there must be a good explanation, but others may not give him the benefit of the doubt.

"What?" Ky demands. "You do not wish to tell me?"

"It's not that," I say. "You are just very close with Tutan and …"

"And you do not trust me," he says, anger erupting in his voice. "I am not a child, Sesha!"

"I know … Ky!" I call after him, but he has already spun around and is stalking off, leaving me very much alone despite the merriment carrying on around me.

29

DISTRESSED AT MY QUARREL with Ky, I head to the infirmary, which at the moment resembles Pharaoh's zoo, full of creatures in all shapes and sizes emitting a variety of squawks, grunts, and cries. Ahmes is organizing the patients into different areas. Those with digestive issues from overindulging or other minor complaints are to go to one corner. Those who have taken too much blue lotus flower go in another. Anyone suffering from any type of wound or accidental injury, perhaps from attempting an acrobatic stunt better left to the professionals, goes to another area.

Reb is examining the tooth of a man who bit into a plum pit too vigorously. He seems to prefer working with teeth. Distractedly, I wonder if he will choose that as his specialization? After our oaths are taken, we will spend another year specializing in a particular area of the body. I have not yet thought about what I will focus on, but I am drawn to surgery like my father before me.

Paser does not acknowledge my presence after I return from my confrontation with Ky. Guilt stabs me in the gut, as if I, too, like some of the patients, have overindulged in rich foods. Is Ky right about my inability to trust people? Though it is not as if I do not have good reason. Unable to ignore inner nigglings of self-reproach, I let out a sigh. I suppose this means there are two to whom I must apologize tonight.

Looking for an excuse to approach my friend, I wonder how best to address the matter. Directly, like Paser himself, I expect. Spotting a jug of water, I pick it up and carry it over to where he is tending the blue-lotus takers. Most of his patients are just lying around looking dreamy and he sends the ones who seem all right on their way. Used to induce a state of higher consciousness, the flower's main effects are sedative, but those who take too much, combined with an excess of alcohol, are at risk of dehydration, especially after a long day in the hot sun.

He nods his thanks, holding a cup out, and I pour the water into it. "I am sorry," I say.

"For what?" he says, passing the drink to one of the patients.

"For not telling you that Merat is to be married."

"I am not mad at you, Sesha," he says.

"You're not?"

"You used your judgment and did not think it relevant to tell me." His calm tone contrasts with Ky's angry one, but I am struck by the similarity of their sentiments.

My eyes lock with his dark ones. "Her father has promised her to a Hyksos chief as a diversionary tactic, to placate the Kings of the North, with whom he thinks we might be going to war. It is why he and Wujat need the scroll so desperately. In the event that war does occur, they want to be prepared."

"So Pharaoh is offering his daughter as a token of peace?"

"That is what daughters are for!" one of the large noblemen pipes up, before dropping back into snores.

I throw a cup of water in his face, rousing him as he splutters and coughs. "You are fine. Go find somewhere else to sleep where you will not drain our time and resources unnecessarily."

Too woozy to protest much, he lumbers to his feet and stumbles off, alternating between grumbling at his poor treatment and giggling at who knows what. I pray he does not have any daughters.

"Let us forget this matter," Paser says, handing a cool cloth to one of his patients. "It is only my pride that has been slighted, and I understand your reasons." He gives me an acknowledging smile and for a fleeting second I wonder if there is another reason why I did not say anything of Merat's engagement. "Where did you put the scrolls?" he asks, lowering his voice, and I push down jumbled feelings, like overflowing laundry into a woven basket, mentally placing the lid on top. And a large stone on top of that. Now is not the time.

"I left them in Ahmes's quarters. He will study them over the next few days before performing the surgery." That is, if Ky will let him. I must figure out a way to convince my brother that this is his best option.

"I still cannot believe that your father was transcribing a scroll written by the Great Imhotep himself!" Paser's hushed voice is full of awe.

"I know." It confounds my mind to even think of the priceless document wrapped in the luxurious shawl, sitting behind the chest of surgical instruments.

Reb walks over. "Sesha, there is someone here asking for you."

I look up to see Kewat standing there. Her face is ashen. Quickly, I walk over.

"What is the matter?" I ask. Her face grimaces with pain.

"Something is wrong. I … I have some bleeding," she says, looking fearful.

"How much?" Immediately, I take her arm and look for a semi-quiet spot where I can have her lay down. Bleeding heavily in pregnancy is never a good sign, though a little here and there is common. But it is still very early and the highest chance of losing the baby is during the first three moons.

Spotting an empty mat, I help her to recline and do a brief examination. The blood seems to have stopped for now.

"You must rest and do very little work. Perhaps it is time you let your mistress know your situation." I push a piece of dark hair back from her pale brow. "And what of the father? Should I send for him?"

"No," Kewat says, her dark eyes wide. "He does not know yet."

"All right. Wait here. I will get you something to ease the cramping." Standing, I look for Ahmes, who is by the table full of medicines, barking out orders and directing people here and there.

"Ahmes," I say. "Do we have any cinnamon bark?"

"Yes, in the amber bottle just there."

"Thank you." I grab the bottle and turn to go back to Kewat.

"Did you manage to find your brother?" Ahmes calls after me.

"Yes." I turn, forcing a smile to my face. "He was excited by the news of our discovery." Though not so much about an upcoming operation.

"I must say, Sesha, you have found an incredible treasure." Ahmes looks at me with respect. "Your father would be proud of you. In addition to your skills as a fine physician."

"Thank you, Ahmes," I say, bowing to him, touched at his words. Threading my way back through the moaning masses I think of the incredible treasure my father had been hiding. Does anyone else know about the artifacts in the secret room? And if not, what had he meant by not revealing its secrets? I need to find out more. Pharaoh and Wujat will want to know where the scroll came from, and I do not want my father's memory further tainted with rumours that he might be a thief.

Exhausted after my shift, I return to the main areas where the party is still in full swing. Some are taking a temporary reprieve from making merry and are slumbering wherever a free spot can be found. I make my way to the inner room where the royal family is holding court.

There are some loud shouts and a large man with a thunderous expression storms past.

"May Ammit the Devourer take your souls!" he yells, waving a burly arm. Barely managing to avoid being knocked over by the massive foreign dignitary, I wait for some semblance of calm to return to the room — the man's abrupt and profanity-filled exit has caused quite a commotion.

I slip into the room as unobtrusively as possible, looking around for Ky, hoping to spot him curled up with Tutan somewhere.

"Leave my sight at once!" Pharaoh points and shouts at Merat, whose expression blazes with defiant fury. She runs from the room, head held high, but I see the unshed tears on her face, being familiar with them myself. Queen Anat casts an indecipherable look at her husband and follows. I look for something to hide behind, but am exposed.

"Sesha!" Pharaoh says, heat still in his voice. "What is it you want? Have you come to tell me you have found the scroll?" he demands.

"I am very close, Your Highness." I drop my eyes low, hoping he will not see the truth in them.

"Good." He takes a drink from his golden goblet. "Because it appears we need it now, more than ever."

"Why is that, My King?" I hazard, looking around for Wujat, but he, like Ky, is nowhere to be seen.

"My daughter has rejected the Hyksos chief's proposal." Pharaoh rubs a hand over bleary eyes. "To his face, no less." He takes another gulp of his wine and lowers his voice, the drink loosening his tongue but not his discretion. "And once the people realize that there is no food there will be much civil unrest."

"No ... food?" I falter, looking around at the copious amounts of it. "But I thought you proclaimed the harvest will be plentiful this year?"

Pharaoh's face is bleak. "I have exhausted our current supplies for the festival celebrations, in a final attempt to beseech the gods. Let us pray they have mercy on us. Wujat is confirming, but it appears the water levels are not where they should be. Unless the rains come we will be dealing with famine and — once the Hyksos sense any weakness — war." He looks at me. "I may not be able to control the weather, that is up to the gods, but I will do whatever is in my power to mitigate the costs of battle. The scroll will do that, Sesha. I need it. At once."

The griping is back in my guts. For the love of Isis. I had hoped for more time.

30

"THE SURGERY WILL HAVE to be tonight," I say to Paser as the sun rises in the east, Ra ready to make another trip over the black land. I wonder what the gods think, witness to our human lives and problems. Do we entertain them? Or do they pity us?

"You must let Ahmes know," Paser says.

And there is the small matter of finding my brother, as well.

"He is exhausted and will need his wits about him for the surgery. I will let him rest and finish transcribing the rest of the document myself," I say. "And I need you to do something for me."

"What is it?"

"You must try to find out if any of the other priests know of the hidden room, without giving anything away."

"Why would you think I am capable of that?"

"Because I have faith in you," I say. "It might be the reason my father was killed." Despite the threats of drought and war, I, like Pharaoh, can do little about those things and must focus on what I *can* do. On what I can learn. Disorder looms on the horizon and I must find out what I can before it breaks loose. Maybe my father was protecting the ancient artifacts? Robbery has always been rife in the tombs. And many times it is because certain people were bribed to look the other way. Or help out. Who knows best how and what to steal than the people who put the objects there in the first place?

Something else occurs to me. "There was a scribe named Qar," I say. "See if you can find out what illness he suffered from. Quietly."

"I will do what you ask," Paser says finally. "You can trust me, you know."

"I know," I say, clasping his hand in thanks. "Thank you, my friend."

I walk quickly down the halls, feeling as if I have taken some blue lotus flower myself. Having slept little, an air of unreality settles around my shoulders like an invisible version of the exquisite shawl I wore earlier. And despite all I have discovered, I go now to finish what my father started. Transcribing the scroll.

Most of the palace lies in slumber and I reach the physician's quarters with no concerns. Closing the door behind me, I go to the spot where we hid the priceless artifact and carefully remove it, hoping Ahmes has had adequate time to study. It will have to be enough. The bright sun lights my father's old chambers, illuminating the scrolls as I unroll them, both precious for different reasons.

It is my first time alone with the ancient document, and my breath is taken at its beauty, but also at its significance. Opening my palette, I select a brush and continue transcribing where my father left off. Finishing a sentence here, a description there, copying what I can from the original, I do not stop for food or water. My hand steadily dips my reed into the black and red paints, fine hairs soaking up the pigment, then transferring it to my father's papyrus.

The morning passes quickly as I block everything else out and write, write, using all my knowledge and skill, everything I have learned. The front of the scroll lists almost fifty cases of injuries, dislocations, tumours, fractures, and other types of fascinating wounds. Each case details the examination of the patient, and their diagnosis, prognosis, and treatment. I am amazed at how comprehensive the manual is. The knowledge it contains is extraordinary; I can see why Father wanted to protect it, the reason for all the secrecy. He wanted to safeguard it, not only because it is a treasure for our time and those to come, but because the information in it can save lives otherwise doomed. Anyone who has the scroll has a powerful weapon, not only over their enemies, but over death itself. It is no wonder that some of the priests felt threatened.

Aside from a few spells on the reverse side, the scroll is entirely rational, methodical, and scientific in its findings. Father was right. Practical medicine and magic *can* coexist. The spells have an important place in healing. If nothing can medically be done for a patient, then perhaps they will take comfort or find strength in the words and incantations a doctor or priest can offer.

The word *brain* catches my eye. This is what Father must have been referring to. Excitedly, I read about the cranial structures and the surface of the organ. Cerebrospinal fluid. That must be what is causing the pressure in Ky's head! The scroll also mentions the pulsations of the organ and —

"Sesha."

I look up and blink burning eyes at my brother.

"I wish to consult you on the surgery."

I blink again, praising every god who has ever existed. So he is still considering it. "Whatever your questions, I will do my best to answer."

"I had the most vivid dream." Biting the end of my brush, I nod at him to continue. Dreams are sacred and prophetic, a message from the gods. Ky takes a deep breath. "There were two of me, standing on each side of the Nile, blindfolded. I told Tutan and he asked the potion-woman, Nebet, to interpret it."

Ah, so Nebet is not only a sorcerer in terms of enhancing appearances.

"She said there is a big decision I must make, and the choice lies with me," Ky says softly. "But I feel like I am being pulled in opposite directions." He looks down. "If the rumours are true, our father was shunned for choosing medicine over the will of the gods. It may even be the reason for his death."

There are so many things that I want to say to him, all crowding to leave my mouth at the same time. No words are able to break through, leaving me silent.

"Do I trust that the gods know what is best for me and leave my fate to them?" he continues, anguish in his voice. "Or do I take things into my own hands, like our father did, and possibly suffer the same consequences?"

"Ky." One gasping thought finally emerges. "Father believed we should use all the tools at our disposal to save a life. We have these tools now." I gesture at the scroll, forcing myself to speak calmly, not wanting to pressure him unduly but needing him to understand. "The gods would not have aided us in our quest if they did not want you to be saved." He nods slowly, weighing my words, and so I press on. "And Nebet is right; the only thing that matters right now is what *you* think. Not the opinions of others." I give him a crooked smile, a little tremulous. "Though I hope you will take your sister's into account."

His brown eyes look up at me, wide in his small face. "Do you really think I will live?"

"It is your best chance." The words are out before I even consider them. "Your only chance."

He takes a deep breath and inclines his head. "Then, as my father's son, let me trust in medicine as he did. I will have the operation."

"You are very brave, just like him." I blink back tears, unsure if they are from the straining of my eyes or from emotion. Putting down the reed brush, I walk over to Ky and hug him tight. "Do not worry. All will be well, Brother. I feel the spirit of our parents close; they will be with us, guiding Ahmes's hand."

He gives a small nod, lower lip only slightly quivering.

"I am sorry I did not trust you," I add. "You were right. I thought of you only as a child, but now I see you are becoming a young man. If they were here, I know they would tell you how proud they are."

"Well," Ky clears his throat and throws back his small shoulders, striving for casualness, "if things do not go as planned, perhaps they can tell me themselves." He leaves with a wave and a promise to meet back here at nightfall and I sit, light-headed, back down on the stool.

After Ky's reed-splitting decision and disconcerting attempt at humour, my hand shakes too much to finish transcribing the other sections of the document without error, so I roll the scrolls back up, taking a few deep breaths.

He is not wrong. The surgery is dangerous. Ahmes will have to drill a small hole in Ky's head to drain the fluid and release the pressure around the skull. I will administer the poppy milk but he will still feel pain, indeed, may even wake up during the surgery. His arms and legs will have to be strapped down so he does not move involuntarily if this happens.

Am I doing the right thing in encouraging him to go through with it?

I shudder to think of my brother lying there — restrained, cut open, most likely in intense pain — and walk to the small window. It is almost midafternoon. The festivities will begin picking up again soon. Pharaoh needs the scroll. There is the threat of famine. We may be on the brink of war. If it is to happen at all, it has to be now. I breathe in deeply. The winds are light this morning but carry in the smells of food being prepared for the masses.

Courage.

The word floats to me on the soft breeze, caressing my face. It is the third time I've felt my parents' *Ba* speaking to me. Three is a number with great significance — perhaps their spirits are not lost after all. I think of my conversation with Ky, about speaking of them often, and feel comforted. As long as we remember them, they are here with us.

Resolutely, I go back to the scroll. Pharaoh will want the higher priests to officially transcribe the document, maybe even Wujat himself. They need not know about my copy.

"So we are about to declare war and everyone is celebrating?" Reb asks in disbelief.

"Might as well give them one last party," Paser says with his usual infallible grin. He's not aware of the potential food shortages, but even if he were, nothing ever seems to suppress his spirit for long. Though I wonder if learning of Merat's failed engagement has anything to do with his joviality.

She is here now. "My father will not want to worry his people until he is ready to announce his campaign," she says, and I wonder if she knows of the vulnerable harvest. I plan to tell them after the surgery, not wanting to distract them at this critical moment. We are all gathered in the physician's quarters in preparation. Everything is ready. Everyone is here.

Everyone except Ky.

I eye the sinister-looking device that will be used to burrow into his skull and cannot say I blame him for his hesitancy. Ahmes is going over his tools, memorizing their exact placement, testing a blade here, touching an instrument there, quietly murmuring spells and charms to help him in his surgery. I often saw Father do the same thing to ready himself and focus his mind.

I prepare the sleeping draft for Ky, stirring the gummy brown concoction over a low flame. The smell is strong and I am careful not to inhale the fumes. *Where is he?* All our preparations will be for naught if he doesn't show soon.

There is a large clatter down the hallway and some raised voices. Prince Tutan bursts into the room, half carrying Ky, whose left arm is draped around his shoulders. He sags heavily against the young royal, who staggers under Ky's weight. Anubis circles around them, whining.

"He had another attack," Tutan gasps out. I race over to the pair and help Ky to stand, but he is already regaining some of his strength and manages to stand on his own.

"I am all right," Ky says, voice small, glancing around the room with a dazed expression.

"Ky." Ahmes walks over and rests his hands gently on my brother's shoulders. His manner is calm and authoritative. "Are you well enough, my child? I am confident, after examining the scroll, that the operation has an excellent chance of success. But you must be sure."

Ky straightens and looks from Ahmes's face to mine, one hand resting on top of Anubis's head. "I am in good hands, Ahmes," he says, with the bravery of a thousand bulls. "I am ready."

Scooping the potion out of the pot, I walk it over to Ky, who has sat on the table. He takes the large ladle from my hand and swallows a healthy mouthful, making a face at the taste as an involuntary shudder runs through his body.

I take his hand, looking fiercely into his eyes. "I am with you, my brother, and so are Father and Mother; I can feel them here." He nods, his pupils dilating slightly as the medicine begins its work. I give him another drink and rest him back so he is fully reclined on the table. Paser and Reb bind his arms and legs while I stroke his brow, murmuring soothing words and incantations to relax him further. His eyes flutter shut and I look up at Ahmes, who stands there, ready with his instruments. Nodding, I bend low and put my mouth to Ky's ear. "I will not leave your side." But his breathing is deep and even and my words go with him into the land of dreams. Anubis gives another low whine, pads around in a circle and lies under the table.

I look up at Ahmes. "May the gods guide your hands."

31

THE OPERATION IS A SUCCESS.

At least for now. Only time will tell if the procedure will improve Ky's long-term prognosis. I look at my brother, sleeping in Ahmes's chambers, head swathed in white linen bandages. He moves restlessly; one side-effect of the poppy is the vivid dreams it gives. Grinding up the flowers of the blue lotus with the mortar and pestle, I prepare an infusion. There is a lot of it around the palace at the moment and its sedative effects are milder than the poppies' — it will gently ease Ky off the latter.

Evening is once again approaching and the celebrations are picking up anew. I broke the news about the desperately needed harvest, which Merat had suspected, and the others have gone to rest after the combined effects of the surgery and the troubling revelations.

Ky makes a fitful noise in his sleep and immediately I am at his side. Anubis lifts his head, eyes attentive. I do not want to wake my brother to administer the blue lotus just yet. It is imperative that he not move so soon. Scanning the room, my eyes fall on the journal Merat gave me. I brought it with me earlier, thinking I might have another look at it while waiting at Ky's bedside. Picking it up, I examine the writings within. Though much of it still does not make sense to me, the sections that I am able to decipher are full of humour and wisdom. It is easy to see how Qar and Father were friends; they must have been, for the scribe to first show him the scroll. Paser was unable to find out much information about the man's death, only that he was quite old and his illness came on suddenly, which Wujat already mentioned. I try to picture the scribe, but everyone at temple looked similar and I had been shy with them.

A short and ancient elder, with skin as wrinkled as a lizard's, is taking shape in my mind when there is a noise in the hallway and the door bursts open. Nebifu stands there looking around the room. His eyes land on me.

"Where is Ahmes?" he demands. "Pharaoh has need of him."

I stand, not shy now. "I do not know. I have not seen him these past notches on the sundial."

His gaze falls on Ky. "What ails him?"

"A minor wound, Your Holiness," I say with a feigned careless gesture, not wanting to arouse his curiosity. His eyes go to the document in my hands and his face pales as if his lifeblood has been drained.

"Where did you get that?" His voice is a whisper.

"I, um, a friend gave it to me," I say.

"Who?" he insists.

Exhausted from the day's events, I do not have the energy to lie.

"Princess Merat." There is nothing he can do to her anyway.

His face whitens even further and the prickly feeling at the back of my neck increases.

"No," he murmurs. "How …"

Just then there is more noise outside the chamber. It sounds as if there is an entire regiment out there. I prove to be correct when Pharaoh bursts into the room, his personal guard behind him. I rush to Ky's bedside, ready to defend him with only an old scroll if necessary. Anubis jumps to all fours and lets out a cautionary growl. Not only an old scroll, then.

"Nebifu, have you found Ahmes? I must ask —" He notices Ky and me. "Sesha, what is happening here?"

"Your Highness." I bow. Worry for Ky has me offering up the only thing that I know will distract his attention. "I have found the scroll."

"Is this true?" He advances toward me. Reaching far back into the shelf, where I placed it after the surgery, I extract the document and present it to the king, kneeling, scroll held aloft. With a sudden intake of breath, he takes it from my hands, eyes shining, and examines the writing.

"Praise the gods, Sesha! Well done!" His excitement is palpable. "Where did you find it?"

"At the temple," I answer honestly. Ky emits a small moan from his bed, stirring.

"The temple?" Pharaoh looks incredulous. "But Wujat searched there thoroughly." It occurs to me to wonder where Wujat is. It is not often that he is not by his king's side.

"It was in a room of untold riches, hidden underneath in the catacombs," I blurt out, with a defiant look at Nebifu. His eyes shoot daggers.

"Hidden riches? How is it that I do not know of this room, Nebifu?" Pharaoh asks in a tone as hard as stone. "These items could be used to pay for the campaign, or supplies!"

"Your Highness," Nebifu says, waving an arrogant hand in that manner he has, "allow me to explain …"

"What do you wish to explain? That you were concealing critical information? Information that we have been desperately seeking? That you lied to your king?" Pharaoh says, eyes cold. "What else have you deemed unworthy of mentioning?"

My eyes widen at Pharoah's implication that this is treasonous behaviour. I swallow. It is not so different from my own.

"The High Priests are sworn to protect the ancient treasures of Egypt," Nebifu protests. "There are worrisome times ahead. Any fool can see that. We were only trying to secure the most priceless artifacts of our past."

Pharaoh's voice drops to a level as dangerously low as the Nile. "Are you calling me less than a fool? Suggesting that I am unfit, or that I cannot see what is best for my land and my people?"

"Much has already been squandered," Nebifu whines, one hand going to the collared necklace he wears. "Paying tribute to placate the foreign rulers in the North ..."

Pharaoh exhales strongly through his nostrils. "I will deal with you later. But for now" — he motions to the soldiers — "arrest him."

"No! You are making a mistake!" Nebifu shouts as the guards seize him.

Pharaoh ignores him and turns to me. I remain frozen. "Thank you for this, Sesha." He holds up the scroll. "You have done your nation and your king a great service." Turning on his heel he leaves the room. Nebifu is still resisting, struggling futilely with the guards.

"Daughter of Ay," he calls as they drag him out of the room, "your father was sworn to protect the treasures of Egypt. You must finish his work and see them safe!"

And then we are alone. My mouth hanging open in shock, I look over at Ky, who is sitting up and rubbing his eyes.

"Sesha?" he croaks, as Anubis lets out a joyful yelp. "What is happening? I had the strangest dreams."

After giving Ky the infusion and reassuring him that all is well and that he must rest, I pace the room, at a loss as to what I should do. Nebifu's words have made me feel like I've ingested the poppy myself, unsure of what is real and what is not.

"Why do you not just go and speak with him?" Ky says, licking his lips, voice cracking. Rushing to his bedside, I hold a cup of water while he drinks.

"Nebifu? And how would I do that?" I ask. "Go to the Place of Confinement?"

"Why not?" his voice is sleepy as he starts to drift off again.

"I will not get past the guards," I say. "And you need me here, with you."

"I will stay with him." I look up to see Merat enter the room. I wonder how much she has heard. Her cheeks are flushed, but never has she looked more beautiful. "But you must go now, while everyone is occupied with the celebrations," she says, waving me off. Inhaling deeply, I feel dizzy from the residual fumes of all the medicines that I have prepared of late.

"Go, Sesha," Ky murmurs from the table. Making up my mind, I nod.

"Thank you, Princess," I say to Merat, bowing low.

"What are friends for?" she says, with a slight smile.

Bending, my hands come up to scratch behind Anubis's ears. "Watch over him," I whisper into his torn one, then stand. Quickly turning, I take my own copy of the scroll from its place. I gave only the original to Pharaoh, some instinct telling me to keep the nearly finished copy to myself, even with Ky's surgery complete. I walk over to my brother, who has settled comfortably into a light sleep, and kiss his forehead.

"I will be back," I say, then turn to leave the room. A thought strikes me and I pause at the doorway, turning to Merat.

"Tell me … friend," I say with a nod to the journal of Qar, still resting at the foot of my brother's bed. "How did you come by that?"

She looks surprised but answers my question.

"My mother gave it to me."

Pondering Merat's words, I steal down the corridors of the palace. The celebrations are set to be even more raucous than the night before.

My mother gave it to me.

I leave the warm glow of the palace and make my way through the dark to the Place of Confinement, where the occasional prisoner is kept. Punishment is typically dispensed swiftly, with offenders either being fined, losing an ear or limb, or being immediately put to death, depending on the severity of their crime. Will Nebifu answer my questions? That is, if he is still capable of doing so — the cutting out of tongues being another popular chastisement for wrongdoers.

No. Pharaoh is a lenient man. He will at least wait until the festival is over before dispensing justice. Though he will not look kindly on what he assumes to be betrayal, Nebifu is still the High Priest. Whatever happens to him, it must be dealt with in a fair and just manner.

I am getting close. As I leave the crowds of loud revellers far behind, it is quiet. And dark. Swallowing, I quicken my pace, wishing I had Anubis for company.

"Got you!" a harsh voice growls in the night, and my arm is grabbed sharply. I gasp at the pain. "Look who it is. Our little Flea." The fruit vendor sneers at me, his breath as rancid as ever.

"We have been watching you," his wife's voice floats out of the darkness, and the malice in it makes me shiver. "And here you are, presenting yourself like a stuffed quail at a feast."

"Let me go," I demand, trying to keep the fear from my voice. "I am on the pharaoh's errand."

"I do not think so, Flea," says the vendor with a spit to the ground. "We have bided our time long enough. Now, you will pay for your thieving treachery."

"What treachery?" I cry out, anger overtaking fear. "For taking some food to feed my starving brother? Have you no compassion?"

The vendor pulls up short, looking at his wife. "What say you?" he asks running the knife in his hand slowly along her arm. "Have we any compassion?"

She shivers, eyeing me intently, a smile playing about her lips, like that of a cat who knows she has the mouse well trapped between her paws.

"None at all, I'm afraid," she purrs. Wrenching my arm hard, they drag me off the path. I scream then, not in fear, but in white-hot rage that I will not get to ask Nebifu my questions. I will not find out what happened to my parents. And I will not be back for Ky.

There is a sudden, dull *thud*. The grip on my arm relaxes as the vendor's eyes roll up in his head and he crashes to the ground like a tree being felled. His wife looks around frantically, but too late, as a twin brick catches her swiftly on the side of her temple. She slumps to the ground and I am left standing, panting, my heart pounding so hard I assume it must be visible beneath my robe.

"That man really has the most offensive breath," Reb says, face appearing in the dark. He casts a disdainful look down at the vendor he has just knocked unconscious. "His oral hygiene must be atrocious."

"You can show them the correct way to clean their teeth when they come to," Paser says, coming out of the shadows. He looks down at the vendor's wife, a small contusion forming at her temple. "But I'd imagine that Sesha will want to be on her way."

Throwing my arms around both of them, I give out a stifled sob. "Thank you."

"There will be time for thanks later," Reb says. "For now, let us go and speak with my uncle."

32

"**W**HERE DO YOU THINK he is being held?" Paser whispers. We are in the City of the Dead, back on the west bank of the Nile. We walk through the necropolis, not toward the ancient tombs where my parents lie, but straight ahead, toward the cliffs.

"In one of the pits," I say. After a moon of associating with all sorts of characters, I had heard of the place. It is where you are kept while your fate is being decided, and more often than not, left to rot, forgotten, especially if there is no one to petition for your freedom. We approach a large hole, at the base of the cliffs, and I peer over the edge. It is black and I can see nothing.

"Is anyone down there?" I call, as loudly as I dare.

A strange tongue greets our ears, frantic and beseeching.

"Who is *that*?" Reb asks.

"It must be the Hyksos spy they captured," Paser says. "I am surprised he is still alive."

"Pharaoh probably did not want to anger Merat's betrothed," Reb mutters.

"More likely, they did not get all the information they wanted," I say, wiping damp palms on my robe. Walking over to another pit, I try again. "Your Holiness?" I whisper.

"Yes?" A voice cries out eagerly. "Who's there?" Praise the gods.

"It is I. Sesha."

"Sesha, you must free me."

I look around. There is a large rope coiled to our right. Grabbing an end, I dangle it enticingly, but well out of Nebifu's reach.

"First you must answer some of my questions," I say, desperation making me ruthless. I push the feeling aside. It is time to learn the truth.

"What is it you wish to know?" His voice is impatient.

"Were you stealing from the pharaoh?"

"No! It is as I said. The High Priests are sworn to protect our most valuable treasures. If there is an invasion or a revolt, who knows what their fate will be?"

"How was my father involved?" I ask.

"He wanted to tell Pharaoh of the room. He was torn about protecting the treasure and keeping secrets from the king. Your father felt that Pharaoh could be trusted with knowledge of the chamber."

"And you did not?"

"It is not a matter of trusting Pharaoh, but of preserving the artifacts in the occasion that something happens to the royal family."

"And in that case, you would be left in command of all the priceless objects. That is most convenient." Another thought strikes me. "What of Wujat? Does he know of the room?"

"Of course, the knowledge is passed on to each High Priest."

"But Wujat is Pharaoh's most trusted companion," I counter. "Why did he not feel that Pharaoh should know of the treasure, but my father did?"

Nebifu hesitates. "Wujat also believed that Pharaoh did not need to be burdened with the knowledge. He has enough to think of at the moment."

"Why did you react to the journal?" I demand, feeling that Nebifu did not fully answer the question but having too many more to dwell on it.

"It was a long-time occupant of the chamber," he answers. "Whoever gave it to Merat also knows of the room."

Queen Anat. I recall the way she fingered the shawl. As if she recognized it. But why would she not have also told Pharaoh about the room? And how did she find out about it? For that matter, how did Qar? I ask Nebifu.

His scorn assaults me from the pit. "Qar was once High Priest." We look at each other in amazement. "He took a new name upon his retirement to live out the rest of his days in humility and peace." Nebifu emits a bitter laugh. "It appears you still have quite a lot of learning to do."

"Did you have my father killed to silence him?" I ask, picturing flames licking the rooftop of our house, feeling their heat.

"No. The fire was nothing more than a tragic accident."

My voice hardens. "I do not believe you."

"I swear it. Now, get me out of here!" His voice is impatient.

Paser and Reb, who have been silent during my questioning of Nebifu, come forward now.

"It sounds like quite the conspiracy," Reb says, one hand coming up to touch the brutal scar on his arm made by the stroke of a lash. "Perhaps we should give him some more time to think on his actions."

"Reb? Is that you, my son?"

"I am not your son." His tone is biting, like the wind that has picked up. Dark clouds roll across the sky and I shiver, sensing Set close at hand again, as I had that day on the way to the village. There is a flash of light in the far-off distance and an echoing rumble that resonates in my bones.

"You are my blood," Nebifu implores.

"You are a traitor," Reb rasps.

Nebifu tries again. "Listen to me, both of you. You are scribes. It is your sacred duty to preserve the cultural treasures of Egypt."

"Our duty is also to our king," Paser says, stepping forward.

"Paser, talk some sense into these two," Nebifu urges, desperate.

"What you are saying has merit," Paser begins. Reb and I look at him. "But who is also to say that it is not an elaborate ruse to pocket a nice little reward for yourself?"

We look at each other. A drop of rain lands on my cheek.

"I do not know what to think," I say. My father wanted to tell Pharaoh of the treasure, which means he trusted him, but Queen Anat and Wujat had not. Then again, Nebifu is claiming it isn't about trust, but about duty.

"You cannot leave me in here!" Nebifu screams and Reb flinches. He walks to the edge of the pit.

"You always told me that my actions have consequences," Reb says, looking down into the darkness. "Yours have no less because of the authority of your position. Maybe more so."

"Reb!" Nebifu hisses. "When I get my hands on you, boy!"

"But you won't." Reb walks over to the rope and throws it in the pit without tying the end to anything. "Not ever again." He looks at us. "Come. Justice is not ours to dispense. That is for the pharaoh and the gods."

Silently, we follow him as he leads the way, away from the frustrated yells and threats of Nebifu.

"Where are we going?" Paser asks. I look up at the angry sky — the storm is moving closer. Instead of relief at the coming rains, there is a growing sense of foreboding.

"To my parents' tomb," I say, patting the scroll in my robes to assure myself it is still there, tucked away, along with the guard's ring I found in the ashes. "I did not have time to finish my copy, but one thing Nebifu said was true. Troubled times are coming. I do not know what will happen to the original or any other copies that are made, but will do what I can to ensure this one survives."

I feel a pang at the unknown fate of the original medical papyrus. Though the priceless document was only in my possession a short time, I feel responsible for it somehow, my scribe's heart yearning to complete the transcription, like my father's did. At least this copy is safe. Thankful, I glance in the direction of the far-off pyramids — it will be our own, slightly smaller, legacy to the world.

"What makes you think the scroll will be secure there?" Reb asks.

"It feels right that it should rest with my father," I say. "His spirit will see it safe. I can retrieve it when times are calmer." Maybe even one day, finish my transcription. Feeling more raindrops, I hunch my shoulders and increase my pace.

"What about all the other riches we found in the chamber?" Paser says as he and Reb hurry to keep up.

"We must trust that Queen Anat and Wujat will keep them safe."

"I wonder why they did not speak of the room to Pharaoh," Reb muses, echoing my thoughts.

"Queen Anat's lineage is long and noble and her father and grandfathers were pharaohs before our time," I say. "These treasures have been in her family for generations. Perhaps she has a more proprietary feeling over them?"

"Perhaps," Paser says slowly, "she did not want them to become casualties of war, whether by ransacking and looting, or through sale to fund the campaign. Though I can't imagine she means to let her people starve if the harvest is poor. How do you think she learned of the room if the secret was kept by the priests?"

"Wujat must have told her," I say. It is the only thing that makes sense. Nebifu was alarmed to see the journal, so he must have assumed that someone in the royal family gave it to Merat, or that she got it herself. Another streak of light snakes across the sky. The rains are almost upon us and I walk even faster. The scroll must not get wet.

"So Wujat told the queen but not Pharaoh?" Reb pants. "Why would he do that?"

"Why does anyone do anything stupid?" Paser says, with an acknowledging grin. "He must be in love with her."

Struck silent by this shocking theory and the need to seek shelter before the storm hits, we race the remaining distance to the tomb where my parents lie. Reaching it just as the skies open, we dive through the entrance, Set's torrential fury finally unleashed.

"There is no guard," I say, brushing the damp off. Aside from the intermittent thundering of the heavens the tomb is eerily quiet. It occurs to me that there were no guards standing watch over Nebifu, either.

"They are likely off celebrating with everyone else," Reb says.

The darkness engulfs us as we enter the main chapel. I feel around the walls for a lantern, knowing that my hands trace over painted murals, though they are impossible to see in the dark.

"I have something," Paser says. I follow the sound of his voice and something is thrust into my arms. "Hold this," he says, handing me what feels like a small terracotta pot.

There is the sound of flint striking flint, one, two, three times, a spark, then another and finally it catches the floating wick of the oil lamp. Carefully, we proceed down the steep shaft, lower and lower into the depths of the earth.

"When exactly is this mastaba due to be filled?" Reb asks, glancing around at the confining passageway.

"I am not sure," I say, holding up the light. I will have to come back for the scroll before that happens. We are almost at the central room, where the hallways with the grand arches of inscribed family names lead off into separate tunnels. "This way." I take the path on my right and walk down the deserted hall, the last footsteps to walk this way my own.

I stop at their room and enter, again, sorely aware that I have brought nothing to offer them.

But wait.

That is not true.

Pulling the transcribed scroll from my robes, I place it on top of my father's coffin.

"Here you are, Father," I say, voice low. "I did my best to complete the work you started. It is not quite finished, but I am afraid it is the best I could manage for now. Guard it well."

Paser and Reb have walked in behind me, and though I have kept my voice quiet and my words rushed, Paser puts a hand on my shoulder. "He would be most proud, Sesha."

"Yes, Sesha," a cold voice says. "Most proud."

33

THE THREE OF US SPIN IN unison, like palace dancers who've spent the last five moons rehearsing.

Queen Anat's statuesque form is lit by the dim light of my lantern, and we stand there, struck dumb by her presence. She moves into the room, two soldiers close behind. On her left I recognize the one holding the torch, as he does me. Crooked Nose. He gives me a smile so twisted it makes his nose seem straight.

Hathor, help me.

"Your Majesty," I say, moving my body to block the scroll from her view.

She does not mince words. "Give me the papyrus, Sesha."

"I gave it to Pharaoh, your husband," I say.

"Not that one," she says, hands on her hips, jewels dangling from her wrists. It is strange, what stands out when one is in the grips of shock. I notice the henna running down Queen Anat's arms, dissolving in the rain. Rich red patterns merge in a design even more abstract than the artist, probably Nebet, originally intended. The rest of the queen is fairly dry; the guards must have shielded her with palm fronds to avoid the worst of the weather. Her next words snap me back to attention. "I want the copy your father made."

"How do you know my father made a copy?" I say.

"Everyone knew." She laughs. A low, ugly sound. "Why do you think he was killed?"

I step in front of Reb and Paser, who have been standing tall in front of me. "You tell me." Their solid presence makes me brave. Maybe foolishly so. "Why would a good man be killed?"

"Your father was a heretic, Sesha. He gave as much credence to science as he did to the gods. Maybe more so. And that is a very. Big. Sin." She saunters forward, hands swinging at her sides. "Against the gods. Against Pharaoh and his family. Against all Egypt." She brings her face close to mine and lowers her voice to a whisper. "And though my husband is a brave man, he is still a man, concerned with glory and the exploits of war. Let that get out to the masses, that their pharaoh and his family are, in fact, mere mortals and not the embodiment of their gods on earth … why, who do you think loses their authority?" Her lips brush against my cheek. "Their power?"

My mouth is dry. "You do."

"Clever child." She gives my cheek a condescending pat and pulls back, examining me. "This is especially true in times of political turmoil. It does not take much to swing the balance of power when civil unrest is brewing. And anything that might cause that balance to shift during these precarious times must be … contained. If people come to believe that it is science that saves them — no matter how small its part — and not their gods, it will only add to the chaos. *Ma'at* would never be restored. You do not want to destroy the balance of the entire universe, do you, Sesha?"

"I am flattered at your opinion of me." I lick my lips and meet her dark eyes boldly, as my world crumbles around me. "So you will destroy a priceless document to preserve the illusion of your power?"

"Oh, Sesha." She *tsks* in a mocking tone. "Our power is not an illusion. It is very real, my dear, and currently all-encompassing." She tilts her head to the side, chin resting on the top of her thumb and index finger, looking very much like she's trying to figure out what to do with me. "I am just ensuring it remains so. Now, move," she commands, pushing me out of the way in a tone that brooks no argument. I stagger to the side as she snatches the scroll up off the coffin, examining it critically. "You have a fair hand, my child. It is a pity the world will never know your talent." Swirling her robes behind her, she strides out of the room, guards at her back, spears remaining pointed at us as they reverse, Crooked Nose still holding the torch high.

"Stop," I say, racing to the door. Halfway down the hallway, she turns, scroll clutched tightly in her hand. "What do you plan to do with it?"

She looks surprised. "Why, destroy it, of course. Along with its brother."

"But your husband needs it! For the war, for his men!"

"The gods will provide for and protect us, Sesha." She smiles, serene. "I can see you are just as your father was, of little faith. I suppose that means you will also have to be ... dispatched."

I ignore her threat. "And what of the other treasures? If the crops fail, they could be used to buy food for the kingdom!"

Her eyes narrow at me. "Funny, your father also felt that feeding the hordes was more important than preserving the precious riches of our nation. He thought my husband could trade some of the less useful items, though the man was quite particular about his papyri." She taps the scroll against a hennaed palm. "Hypocrisy, if you ask me. Expecting me to sell off my family's priceless heirlooms like some pathetic beggar." She laughs in amusement. "The crops will be just fine, Sesha, the Inundation is not over. Even now, Isis's tears fall. Besides, famines come and go — it is an unfortunate, yet handy, way to rid the land of ... excess. My family will be just fine."

"You will doom them all," I shout, Paser and Reb behind me.

"Shh, my child," she says, frowning in annoyance. "You really are most irritating with your opinions. Much like my daughter Merat. Though I suppose she has me to thank for that." She eyes me down her nose like I am a speck of pond scum on the palace pool. "And speaking of Merat, I know you two have become quite close. You should be the first to learn that she was given to the Hyksos chieftain right before I came here, regardless of her protestations. As a token of our good faith." Seeing my face, she gives me a look that makes my blood stop in my veins. "But not to worry, we will take care of Ky."

"Don't you touch him," I growl, barely recognizing the voice as my own.

"That will depend on you, my child. Follow us, and not only will my guards kill you on the spot, but I will have to whip up another batch of that poppy infusion you prepared him. Though I lack your skill, of course, so who knows what else may *accidentally* end up in the concoction. The last person to drink one of my tinctures did not fare so well, I'm afraid. Poor Qar."

With a final swirl of her robes, she departs from the hallway and begins to ascend the shaft. Crooked Nose and his partner sneer and make threatening jabs at us as they retreat after her. My eyes fall on Crooked Nose's hand, the one holding the torch. Unlike his partner's, his finger is missing a ring. A ring I feel pressing into my side, where I've been keeping it at all times.

"It was you!" I shout. "You started the fire! You killed my parents!" I leap at him, dropping my lantern.

Paser and Reb grab both my arms, restraining me from clawing his eyes out. Or rather, more likely, from being skewered like a fish.

He gives me a contemptuous look and bows low. "At your service, Flea. But I cannot take all the credit." Nodding over his shoulder at Queen Anat's retreating form, his tone is almost jovial. "Just following orders." He lets out an ugly chuckle. "Though I can't say I didn't enjoy it."

Snarling and hurling every curse at him that I can imagine only makes him laugh again, his taunting jeers echoing as he and his partner ascend the shaft behind the queen, and — aside from all the mummified bodies — leave us very much alone in the dark.

34

THE FIRST PILE OF RUBBLE to fall down the shaft crashes to the ground in a spray of dust and gravel. Coughing, we run to the shaft, and I yell up it, "You can't seal us in here!"

"On the contrary, Flea, we can." Crooked Nose's voice carries down, along with another shovelful of large rocks, followed by a few large boulders which are obviously being rolled and pushed into the narrow exit. More dust flies. We are being entombed alive.

"What are we going to do?" Reb's voice is panicked. "If we try to go up there we'll end up taking a rock to the head and our brains will look like the ones in Sesha's satchel."

I give him a look. "Thank you for recalling that particular image to my mind, Reb."

"There must be another way out," he insists.

"There is not," I say, through gritted teeth. "That is the whole point of a tomb. One way in, one way out.

Crooked Nose must have been following me the whole time." Mentally, I curse myself for not being more aware, knowing now whose eyes I'd felt, watching me.

"Listen," Paser says. "Do you hear that?"

"What?" I say, morose. I have failed everyone I love.

"Nothing at all," he says, pressing his ear against the wall. "The shovelling has stopped. There is no more rubble falling."

He is right. We race to the exit, waiting cautiously for another hailing of rocks and boulders to come pouring down. It is silent.

"We have to get to Ky!" I shout and bolt up the steep incline.

"Sesha!" Paser shouts behind me. "Wait!"

Paying no heed, I race up the shaft, arms protectively blocking my face, expecting a large and heavy rock to smash into my body at any moment.

Emerging into the chapel, I breathe hard.

Crooked Nose eyes me balefully, shovel on the ground. The other guard must have accompanied Queen Anat back to the palace, leaving only him behind to see to her dirty work.

"Why did you stop?" I ask the sullen soldier, as Paser and Reb rush up the stairs behind me. Not that I am complaining.

"Because I commanded him to," a voice says.

Turning, I see a small form standing there, proud and imposing for all its diminutive height.

Prince Tutan. And behind him, gripping one of his larger surgical blades, Ahmes.

"But how did you know we were here?" I ask. The rains have stopped and the skies are clearing.

"Ky told us you were going to see Nebifu," Ahmes says. "From there Anubis led us." The dog trots out from behind Ahmes, who fondly pats his head.

I feel a spurt of panic for my brother. "But who is with Ky?"

"I believe they said their names were Bebi and Kewat," Ahmes says. "They offered to care for him until my return."

"But Queen Anat … she … she …" Fear stabs at my heart. I have filled Ahmes in, while Paser and Reb gave a slightly edited version to Tutan. We do not need the young prince on the defensive, or pressured to choose between us and his mother.

"She will not be concerning herself with a young boy at this precise moment," Ahmes says, softly. "There are other more important matters for her to attend to."

"My mother will not hurt my friend," Tutan says, overhearing. But a dubious expression crosses his face as he contemplates his words. "Come," he bids Crooked Nose. "Let us return to the palace." Reluctantly, the soldier obeys, following his future king and beloved child of his queen, who would be most displeased to hear if anything happened to her only son and heir to the entire kingdom.

I start to follow Tutan and Paser stops me, a firm hand on my shoulder. "Sesha." His tone is gentle. "We cannot go back to the palace."

"I must. Ky needs me."

"He is well, Sesha, and under my care," says Ahmes. "Besides, you know Anubis will let no harm come to him." He allows a brief smile, which fades. "But Paser is right. The queen will not want you interfering in her plans."

"And what plans are those, exactly?" I ask.

"I am not sure," Ahmes admits. "But it does not escape my attention that if something were to happen to Pharaoh in battle, Tutan will become king, effectively making Queen Anat ruler of the land as his regent. Have no fear, your escape will go unmentioned." He nods at Crooked Nose's back. "He will not want her hearing of this."

"But what of the scroll?" My heart despairs at the loss of the papyrus. My father's legacy. Our legacy. "Pharaoh has need of it." The world has need of it.

"Leave it, Sesha," Paser says.

"Do not worry," Ahmes says. "I'm Pharaoh's physician — who do you think he will entrust the document to? I may be able to make another copy without the queen's knowledge and will do what I can to protect the original." His words alleviate some of my distress.

"And where are we to go, what are we to do?" Reb interjects. "As you say, Ahmes, if we go back now, the queen will have us killed."

Though my heart breaks a little at the thought of not seeing Ky in the immediate future, I bind it tightly with strips of resolve.

"Then we must go north. To the Hyksos kings." I look at Paser and Reb, gauging their response to my radical proposition. "I have a feeling that Merat might like to see a familiar face. Or three." Our skills as physicians will be valued in an upcoming battle and may provide an adequate cover for rescuing her. More likely we will be killed on the spot, but I cannot let my friend be given away like some conciliatory trinket.

"North?" Reb echoes, looking like he is stuck in quicksand.

"North," Paser agrees with a nod, folding his arms over his broad chest.

"Take this." Ahmes hands the blade to Paser before turning to face me.

"Thank you, for everything," I say to him. He clasps my hand like I am his equal, bringing it to chest height, his other hand covering our grip. "The girl, Kewat. She is with child. Care for her."

He nods. "May the gods protect you, Sesha." His eyes scan me, anticipating the words I am about to say. "And have no worry for Ky. I will see that he is safe." Anubis barks in agreement.

"I know," I say. He releases my hand and turns to leave the mastaba.

"Ahmes."

He stops at the exit and looks over his shoulder. The lantern on the wall flickers, casting a glow on the Day of Judgment scene inscribed on the wall, flames illuminating our patron god, Thoth, reed brush poised in his hand.

"Tell my brother I will be back for him." My voice is as unwavering and steadfast as the Great Pyramids. "And the scroll."

Author's Note

THE EDWIN SMITH MEDICAL PAPYRUS (the "secret scroll" Sesha seeks and transcribes) is a real-life document! A manual of military surgery and the oldest known treatise on trauma, it was discovered by tomb robbers and sold into the hands of Edwin Smith, a rare antiquities dealer in the late 1800s. His daughter later recognized its extreme importance and donated it to the New York Museum of Medicine in the early 1900s, where you can see it today. The scroll is believed to be dated to the SECOND INTERMEDIATE PERIOD (approx. 1650–1550 BCE) and is assumed to be a copy of a much older medical document attributed to the Great Imhotep, Egypt's first renowned physician, scribe, Grand Vizier, and High Priest (among many other things). The copy is believed to have been written by two scribes, with the second making small additions that are incomplete in some sections, as if the scribe were interrupted mid-transcription …

Not only is the scroll one of the world's most priceless artifacts, it is also important because it is the first document that demonstrates a rational and scientific approach to medicine, rather than relying solely on magic and superstition.

The book is set during the Second Intermediate Period, one of the most obscure periods of Ancient Egyptian history and during which the country fell into disarray. The Hyksos, "rulers of foreign lands," gained control over the Nile Delta and ruled from the port city of Avaris (modern Tell el Dab'a). Egyptians viewed this brief period as a blight on a glorious history, but it was actually thanks to the Hyksos (who — for the most part — held an uneasy truce with Thebes), that new advancements, particularly in weaponry and military procedures, were introduced to the Egyptians, allowing them to eventually take back their lands and heralding in the extraordinary era of the New Kingdom. Even now, new research is being carried out and there are proponents of several theories regarding this tumultuous time, as the world's renowned Egyptologists attempt to unlock the mysteries of the past and decipher its stories.

Writing historical fiction is always a bit tricky, as the writer desperately wants to get it right for the audience, but it's especially challenging when a book is set over 3,500 years ago! Some things we know, but many more things we don't. There are differing theories, perspectives, and assumptions made when examining the past, and researchers have to be aware of the lens through which they view the world. Even our language shapes the way we think! This book is a work of fiction and while I tried to get the details as accurate as years of research allowed, I hope what you take away is a passion and respect for the great civilizations that came before us. I would love for this series to inspire you and other young readers to get excited about history and to explore it for yourself, unearthing your own thrilling adventures and stories along the way. But while you do, be mindful of your own "lens" that you look at the world through, and remember that other people have their own lenses, too. We are all brothers and sisters who share a home called Earth, and we must do what we can for it, and for one another.

Xoxo, Alisha

ACKNOWLEDGEMENTS

IT TRULY DOES TAKE A VILLAGE to write a book, a process that involves years of research and writing. I am fortunate to have many wonderful people in my village whose efforts and contributions helped make this story possible. I could not have written *Scroll* without the support of my husband, Aaron, who was also one of the manuscript's most ardent fans. To Angela Misri, whose initial idea for another project sparked the ember for this story, and to my writer friends Meaghan McIsaac, Joyce Grant, and Ainslie Hogarth for their encouragement and complete understanding of how crazy a writer's life can be.

To Ali McDonald and Olga Filina, for believing in the manuscript and getting it into the hands of the right people. To everyone at Dundurn Press, including Scott Fraser, who championed the book, as well as Kathryn Lane and Jenny McWha from the editorial team, and my incredible editor, Jess Shulman. A giant thank you to art director Laura Boyle for overseeing this stunning cover and to superstar illustrator Queenie Chan for bringing Sesha's world to life.

To Egyptologist Roberta Shaw for sneaking me into the Royal Ontario Museum's private stacks to do research, and to the Ontario Arts Council, whose literary grants contributed to the creation of this book.

To my friends and family who support me and my writing — thank you for everything. And, as always, to my children, Aira and Nolan, I love you, keep reading, and keep dreaming.

And, finally, to you, the reader. Thank you for spending some of your very precious time with Sesha and her friends on this adventure; I hope you will be back for the next one.

Coming Summer 2020 ...

THE
DESERT
PRINCE

Book 2 in the Secrets of the Sands series